IN A LEAGUE
OF THEIR OWN

IN A LEAGUE OF THEIR OWN

MILLIE GRAY

BLACK & WHITE PUBLISHING

First published 2010
by Black & White Publishing Ltd
29 Ocean Drive, Edinburgh EH6 6JL

1 3 5 7 9 10 8 6 4 2   10 11 12 13

ISBN: 978 1 84502 284 6

A CIP catalogue record for this book is available from the British Library.

Typeset by RefineCatch Ltd, Bungay, Suffolk
Printed and bound by Cox & Wyman, Reading

AUTHOR'S NOTE

This story tells of one family's life in Leith and the Hebrides in the 1950s. Although it echoes some of the writer's experiences and personal feelings, the characters portrayed in the book are wholly fictitious and bear no relation to any persons, living or dead. Many of the street names, localities and other details from that period in Leith's history have been preserved however.

To Gordon Booth in acknowledgment of all his
help and encouragement

1
A MERRY DANCE

In sheer frustration at Alice's inability to perfect the rhythm and steps of the Charleston, Carrie emphasised once again to her younger sister, "No, no, Alice! Let the music guide you. See? Like this." And Carrie continued to sing and dance in time to the music. "Dah, dah! Dah-dah, dah-dah, ah, ah." Unfortunately, the only response from Alice to this advice was a half-hearted flick of her right leg followed by a clumsy twirl of her long beaded necklace. Carrie skipped across the room and brusquely switched off the record player. "No, no!" she remonstrated. "When you do the high kick – and that was meant to be a *high* kick you were attempting – then it's a half-flick first followed through with the full kick."

A crestfallen Alice whimpered, "I *am* trying, Carrie."

"You most certainly are *very* trying," was the sarcastic retort from Carrie who still couldn't understand why Alice was not, like herself, one of nature's natural movers. Mellowing her tone she continued, "Look, I thought that with all the dancing lessons you've had, the Charleston would be a cake-walk for you."

"Well, it isn't!" snapped Alice.

"Okay, keep the heid," her sister riposted, demonstrating yet once more just how the dance should be done. "See. After the high kick, you're on to pivoting on the ball of your right foot, kicking out before stepping back, and then twisting on your left foot: dah, dah, and stepping forward. Now, come on – try it in time with me."

Both girls halted abruptly as the front door opened and their brother, Sam, came in. He had sprouted to six feet during his two years in the army, and this, coupled with his sun-enhanced complexion and the signs of grey flecking through his red-tinted hair, made him now appear a quite dominant figure to his sisters.

"Where in the name o heavens d'ye think ye two are going, all dressed up like a couple o Rose Street tarts?"

"You know perfectly well that we're going as the Roaring Twenties Girls to the Halloween fancy dress ball in the Leith Assembly Rooms tomorrow," Alice countered as she retreated safely behind her sister.

"Roaring Twenties? Seems to me it's a burning shame that two well brought-up lassies are going out to make a laughing-stock o themselves."

"You know something, Sam?" said Carrie as she began to face up to him. "Ever since you came back from Korea you've had a face the length of Leith Walk. Finding fault with everything, so you are. And I wouldn't care," she continued with increased boldness, "but you were only out there two months before the shooting stopped!"

Eyes blazing, Sam bristled angrily. "Aye, that was because when we joined up with the Black Watch we didnae half put the fear o God into them."

Without another word he escaped into the kitchen and sat down at the table, his head between his hands. How, he wondered, could he explain to his family – or indeed to anybody – that, hard as his childhood had been, he would rather it had been twice as tough just as long as he hadn't had to go shooting and killing folk he didn't even know!

No, he admitted, as the memories came flooding back, I'm not really a hard man – no natural-born killer. He was jolted back to reality when the harsh ring of metal being banged on metal reminded him of gunfire. "In the name o heavens, Carrie, what are ye doing, scaring me like that?" he yelled, jumping to his feet in alarm.

"Scaring you? What can be frightening about me beating up a batter?"

Sam shook his head in despair. "Oh, Carrie, somebody just *has* to listen to me."

"Okay. I'm all ears."

Sam sighed and sank down on his chair again but hesitated before finally beginning: "Look. Ye ken I was sent out to Korea as part o my National Service."

Carrie nodded, stopped her batter-beating, and sat down beside him.

"Well, try to understand that Paddy Egan and me were both shit-scared, holed up every night in a stinking foxhole with only a Bren gun for company."

"That all?"

Sam paused again before adding, "Well, aye – if ye dinnae count the thousands o Chinese that were dug in just twenty yards from us."

Without answering, Carrie rose to pour the batter into a baking tin which she placed in the oven. It was only when she turned round to face Sam again that she noticed he was shivering.

"Ken what?" he continued, almost to himself. "All freezing night we had to watch and listen for them coming to get us."

"Must have made the nights seem long," Carrie whispered.

"Long? A bloody eternity it seemed. Only other thing ye could do in that midden was sit and think."

"Think about what?" Carrie was now desperate to keep Sam talking.

"About hame. Going to the game on Saturdays. And about Mammy and you lassies." A long pause followed before he blurted out. "Aw Carrie, we *did* fire on them – but please believe me – only when we thought they were really going to do for us." Sam covered his ears with his hands and groaned, "Oh God, the noise o they guns. The flashes. The screams when we hit them – when we murdered them. Funny thing though – in the morning there were nae bodies lying about."

"There weren't?"

"Naw. Dragged them away in the night they did, so we couldnae dae a heid count."

"And was the daytime any better?"

Sam pushed out his lips and blew on them before answering. "Daytime? Oh aye, it was just dandy if ye were into lookin' forward to being fed pigswill washed down with some stinking water from the bloody river Imjin."

"Mmm," Carrie mused. "But that's not what's really bugging you, is it?"

Sam sighed and shook his head. "Naw."

"So what is't that's getting to you?"

"Paddy," was all Sam could say as he dragged his hand over his mouth. "Ye ken how we grew up thegither."

"Aye, but you both went to different schools."

"So he was Catholic. What of it? Did we no join up every Saturday for a game or twa o football?" retorted Sam, before banging the table with his right fist. "And know something . . . killing that po-faced officer, who had the cheek to tell me that the Korean casualties were light compared with the two world wars, would have been easy for me. Why could he no understand it wouldnae be light for Paddy's mammy? Oh aye, what matters to her and me is that Paddy's no coming hame from a bloody war we shouldnae ever have been in." Carrie stayed silent until eventually Sam muttered, "Aye. And the upper-class asses that sent us out there will still have learned nowt. Naw, naw. Paddy'll no be the last nineteen-year-auld to buy it in some bloody foreign field . . ."

Carrie went over and laid a hand on her brother's shoulder. "There's nothing you can do for Paddy or for his mammy now – except make a success of your own life."

"And how will I do that?"

"For a start you can get stuck into your police job next week," replied Carrie as she took the cooked meal from the oven and dished it up.

Sam nodded. "Aye, ye're right – and I'll be outside most o the time in the polis . . . Mustn't be shut in right now."

"Good thinking, Sam. Now, let's get tucked into our tea before it eats us."

Sam looked up, wondering what Carrie was going on about and then he became aware of the plate in front of him. "Toad in the Hole!" he said with a grin. "Ye minded how I just love Toad in the Hole."

Carrie smiled back. "Well, well. Not only are you back with the living but you also know what you're about to eat."

Before Sam could speak, a loud knock at the front door had Alice running to open it. "It's Senga Glass, Sam. She's wondering if you're in?" she called.

Sam and Carrie both groaned before Sam hoarsely whispered, "Do something, Carrie. I just cannae take Crystal right now."

Carrie chuckled at Sam using the nickname he'd given Senga – who believed he called her Crystal because she shone for him – but Carrie knew it was because she came across as fairly thick. However, before either Sam or Carrie could signal to Alice that she should say that he was out,

Crystal had pushed her way in. "Sam," she burst out. "I was wondering if ye were still game to walk me down to the Halloween dance the morn's night."

"Em, em." Sam floundered as he struggled to think of some kind of excuse. "Well, I cannae really – ye see I've promised Chalky I'd go down with him and his cousin from the Dumbiedykes."

Unable to conceal her disappointment, Crystal tried to coax Sam by stammering, "B-b-but I've told everybody ye're going with me and I'm going as Betty Grable – and so are *four* other lassies from the Bond."

"So?"

"Well Sam, if ye don't go down with me how'll ye ken which Betty Grable is me?"

"Simple," sneered Alice. "After all, I'm sure none of the rest will be ban . . ."

Before Alice could finish saying bandy-legged she was silenced with a warning glower from Carrie who was fully aware that Alice could at times be a bitchy big head. This was due to the family insisting to their blonde, willowy, blue-eyed Alice that she could easily become Miss Scotland some day – provided their mother Rachel ever allowed her to lower herself by entering a beauty competition.

Carrie's intervention failed to stop Crystal realising that Sam would remember that, as a child, she'd had rickets which had left her with slightly bowed legs. And as she looked at him, she thought just how strong, straight and handsome he was. It was this recognition that brought tears of regret to her eyes and all that poor Crystal could do was to bend over and pull her skirt further down over her legs.

Crystal's desperate actions reminded Carrie just how badly she herself had felt before the squints in her eyes were corrected, and she blurted out, "Look, Crystal, why don't you walk down to the dance with Alice and me?"

Wiping her nose with the back of hand, Crystal responded, "Aye, that would be just great – us lassies should all stick thegither."

The three wind-tossed girls were glad to escape the clutches of the blustery gale and find refuge inside the doors of the impressive Constitution Street Assembly Rooms where the Halloween ball was being held. As they brushed the rain from their coats, Alice muttered, "We should have taken a taxi."

"A taxi!" screeched Carrie. "We're here tonight dressed up like a pair of demented hens just so you can win first prize in the Fancy Dress – and you think we should have wasted money on a taxi?"

"Carrie, there's only one prize the night, and it's a tenner!" insisted Alice. "A tenner that would go some way to paying my fare to America. But with my head feathers all drookit and hanging down over my face, winning is no longer a certainty for me."

"You win?" sneered Crystal. "When they judges get a butcher's at *my* wig ye'll have nae chance."

"Says you!" huffed Alice.

"Listen, does that music floating down the stairs no make you want to twinkle?" interrupted Carrie, beginning an impromptu dance. "C'mon, you two . . . let's hand our coats in and get up to the hall to see what talent's around."

It was on the dot of eight when the girls arrived in the hall but since the pubs didn't close until ten there were no men on the dance-floor, except for those who had come with a partner; so Carrie, who couldn't keep her feet still, danced with Alice. Crystal in the meantime took up her customary wallflower pose until Sam and Chalky sauntered in just before ten. Immediately she pounced on Sam and dragged him on to the dance floor, insisting emphatically that even though it was a jive it was most certainly a Ladies' Choice!

By cavorting backwards Sam managed to steer himself to where Alice and Carrie were dancing, landing there just in time to see Alice to do a back somersault before being dragged back smartly between Carrie's legs.

"When did you two become contortionists?" Sam exclaimed admiringly as he watched Carrie begin to twist her slim legs in all directions.

"I thought you were coming with Chalky and his cousin from the Dumbiedykes?" said Carrie, ignoring Sam's comments on the dancing.

"Didnae turn up for some reason," drawled Sam, who was now staring at the hall entrance.

Instinctively turning to see what was holding her brother mesmerized, Carrie was confronted with a vision – a true Rita Hayworth look-alike who could well have given the real Rita a run for her money. And it wasn't just the flowing Titian wig and fluttering eyelashes that were so spellbinding – no, the main attraction was her tantalizing and perfectly-formed bosom. There was so much of it that Carrie knew for sure that this Rita would never fall flat on her face. However, before she could speak to Sam again, the next dance had been announced and Carrie's brother dashed across the floor to whirl a very willing Rita on to the floor. As the music of "Jealousy" thundered out, Sam and Rita's interpretation of the tango brought all the other dancers to a halt. All they could do was gape at a version of the dance that would have made George Raft's tango look positively demure!

"Wherever did he learn to dance like that?" cried Crystal, as Sam's legs shot between Rita's and his head abruptly swivelled round to dance cheek-to-cheek with her.

"Not in my mammy's living room – that's for sure!" exclaimed Carrie, whose cheeks were glowing with embarrassment.

"Then where?"

Carrie couldn't answer that – but she guessed that when Sam had been sent from the front line in Korea to Tokyo for two weeks' rest and recuperation he must have taken full advantage of what was on offer there. That of course included long lie-ins, cooked meals whenever he wanted them and the services of the local geisha girls who were doubtless more than willing to allow him to sample their diverse cultural pastimes!

"Never mind about who taught him and where," fumed Alice. "Don't you realise that yon Rita Hayworth double, that our Sam is flaunting around the room, has just stolen the first prize off me?"

All Carrie and Crystal could do was to glumly agree.

There were another three dances before the interval; and Sam danced every one with Rita. As Carrie watched them growing closer together, she had to stifle uncomfortable feelings of jealousy rising within her. Simply watching them both evoked memories in her of how Will and she had clung to each other as they had danced the night away before he left for his ship. She heaved a sigh, remembering how Will had whispered in her ear the wonderful news of how he'd been offered the post of fifth engineer on a Salvesen's whaling supply ship. "I'll only be away six months," he'd assured her.

That was twenty-three months ago and still he hadn't sailed into a British port. She took some comfort, however, at realising that he just *had* to get home shore leave within the next month or the company would be breaking its own contract terms – one of which was that no sailor would be more than two years away from home.

"Shall we join the queue for refreshments, Carrie?" asked Alice, breaking into Carrie's reverie. "What I mean to say is that ever since you started saving up the deposit for a house, no penny in your purse seems allowed out without a police escort."

Ignoring Alice's caustic observations on her frugality, Carrie casually replied. "Oh yes, we might as well join the queue. You never know: Sam might treat us."

"Sam treat us? When has he ever treated anyone except Mammy? And with her away in the Hebrides with Hannah and not being here when he came home on demob leave, I doubt if even she would get a crumb off him, never mind a nibble at his boiled ham sandwich."

Alice was right. After buying his own tea and gammon-filled delicacy, the only other person he treated was Rita. "Did you see that, Alice?" moaned Carrie as Sam handed Rita her cup of tea and slightly less than half of his own sandwich.

"I did. And just see how she's wolfing into it. Honestly, with teeth that size, I hope Red Riding Hood's not around."

After the break, it was time for the Grand Parade and the fancy dress judging. Alice of course was still sulking and Carrie urged, "C'mon. We still have a chance if we look as if we're enjoying ourselves – but if we Charleston around like we're doing a Death March, we've had it."

The parade stopped and everyone stood silently on the dance floor. Not a sound could be heard as the excitement mounted. Then, as the drum-roll echoed around the hall they all knew that the winner of the biggest prize ever was about to be announced. The bandleader began by saying how difficult the judging had been and how he personally had admired the Roaring Twenties girls. Alice and Carrie beamed with pleasure, believing they were now the winners. Their grins faded however, when he went on to say, "Ladies and gentlemen, by a very small margin, the worthy victor is – Rita Hayworth!"

Rita leapt on to the bandstand and ungraciously seized the two mint-new, crisp five-pound notes from the bandleader's hand before turning and brandishing them in triumph.

"Well, that's that," whimpered Alice. "Guess I'll be nearly twenty-five before I get my American fare together."

Carrie was more philosophical and whispered, as she tucked her arm though Alice's, "Look, I could get you a part-time job as usherette in the Palace Picture House. Just think how much you'd learn watching Fred Astaire and Ginger Rogers dance, not just once but seven times over – if you count the double programme on a Saturday."

By the end of the night both Alice and Carrie had declined offers to be walked home and as they emerged on to the pavement in Constitution Street both of them looked for Sam who should have been ensuring that they were safely escorted across Leith Links. But Sam was nowhere to be seen. Only Chalky and Crystal had followed the girls out of the dance hall.

"Where's Sam got to?" Carrie asked Chalky.

"You'd best go by yourselves," advised Chalky.

"Why?"

"Because he's going to walk that big red-heided trollop home," snorted Crystal.

"You're joking!"

"Naw, Carrie, she's no," retorted Chalky. "Making a right ass o himself he is. Tried to tell him to get a grip but he wouldn't listen. Look, here they come."

Out of the dance hall came Sam with Rita clinging to his arm like a leech.

"You seeing us up the road, Sam?" demanded Carrie.

"Naw. You and Alice go up with Chalky and Crystal. I'll see ye later. I'll no be that long."

Carrie turned on her heel and strode off defiantly. However, Chalky grabbed Sam's arm. "Look, pal I ken ye've been away for two years and that ye're keen to get a click but pass this bag o trouble up and come hame with us. It's for the best."

Sam shook his head and pulled Rita closer to him.

"To hell with ye then! And dinnae ever say I didnae warn ye," shouted Chalky, before trotting off after Sam's sisters.

He had just caught up with the girls as they were turning into Charlotte Street when he grabbed Carrie's arm and announced, "I just cannae let him be made a mug of. I'm away back."

Chalky bounded back round the corner and when he saw Sam and Rita approaching St John's East Church he began to sprint as fast as he could towards them. He had just reached Leith Police Station when Sam noticed him and became aware of the danger Chalky might pose to his beloved Rita. In an effort to protect her, Sam moved quickly in front – not fast enough though – for Chalky's lunge knocked the wind out of Sam who fell against Rita. The poor maiden ended up sprawling on the pavement, legs akimbo, her Titian wig now lying five feet away and her once-perfect bosom producing loud, agonising squeals as it slowly deflated.

Sam sat up and, as he stared at Rita's immaculate short back and sides, he slowly realised that he had been completely hoodwinked.

"What the hell?" he groaned as his sisters and Crystal came running towards him.

"I tried to tell ye the hale night lang and ye wouldnae listen," explained Chalky. "This eejit here is my transvestite cousin, Roger, from the Dumbiedykes. He bet me, so he did, that he could fool you and everybody else at the dance."

Sam rose painfully from the pavement but instead of throwing a punch at Roger he squared up to Chalky. "Ye mean this poof here is your cousin?"

"He's no a poof. Naw, naw! He's just a big Jessie," muttered Chalky, preparing to fend off the blows he knew were about to rain down on him.

Fortunately for Chalky, it was just then that Police Sergeant Duff arrived on the scene, "Hello! Hello! What's going on here then?"

"Nothing," Carrie butted in.

The sergeant turned to Sam. "Heard ye were back, Sam. When are ye bound for your polis training at Whitburn?"

"Well," said Sam, who was terrified that the sergeant would find out how he had been fooled. "I get demobbed Monday coming," he continued. "And the week after that I join the force."

"You couldn't have timed it better, what with our outside-right breaking his leg," the sergeant announced before turning his attention to Roger. "You again?" he snorted. "How often do I have to tell you to stay in the Dumbiedykes and let our A Division lads look after ye?" He now turned back to Sam. "You'll remember him because every time he puts a foot in Leith he ends up with a proper doing-up. And us poor B Division lads end up no only taking him to hospital to be patched up but having to write out an assault report – an assault report," he hissed, prodding Roger vigorously in the chest, "that never goes anywhere because he always drops the charges." The sergeant hesitated then wheeled round to give Sam his full attention again. "Didn't manage to pull the wool over *your* eyes, did he?"

"No," replied Carrie. "It was me that was arguing with him."

"About what?" the sergeant speered.

"About him cheating my wee sister."

Sam winked at Carrie before joining in. "That's right. He was trying to run off with something that wasn't really his."

Roger looked bewildered and then realised what Sam and Carrie wanted. Without further persuasion, he reached into his pink handbag and withdrew the two crisp five-pound notes – which he duly handed to a triumphant Alice.

2
A CHILD IS BORN

Rachel rested her head on the cow's flank as she pulled on its teats. "Well," she said to herself, "this is a lot different from pulling pints – for a start I'd be dressed up to the nines running my own bar in the Queen's, not stuck here in a draughty old byre with leaking wellies and a flapping sou'-wester." She sighed, thinking how her Hannah, although now married and already the mother of a fifteen-month toddler, was still such a dither and causing insurmountable problems with all her shilly-shallying. Oh aye, ten days holiday, with three of them unpaid at that, was all she'd managed to wangle out of the management at the Queen's Hotel where she was manageress of the Dispense Bar. All this leave had been wangled so that she could give Hannah a hand with the new baby – she'd even arranged to have these precious holidays a week *after* Hannah's due date. And here she was with only two days' holiday left, a gale force nine forecast and her awkward Hannah still reluctant to give birth.

The cow suddenly fidgeted and slapped Rachel in the face with its tail, making her wince and knock against the bucket. Trying desperately to steady the pail and save the milk, she slipped off the three-legged stool and landed in the straw.

"You still have not quite got the hang of the milking then?" a drifting, lilting island voice called out.

Turning to discover Ishbel, Hannah's husband's aunt, Rachel beamed a smile to the ancient-looking lady, thinking how fierce and forbidding she had seemed the first time they met. Though just in her mid-seventies, Ishbel had looked to be a hundred at least. Rachel had never before seen such a lined and seemingly weary face but she now knew it was due to Ishbel having been a fishwife, who had followed the herring fleet from port to port ever since she'd been a young slip of a girl. And the finishing touches to Ishbel's leathered skin came no doubt from the Hebridean climate where raging gales and driving rain were near daily occurrences. Rachel knew also that Ishbel's austere appearance, accentuated by her steel-grey hair and sombre black dress, belied the fact that both she and her identical twin, Myrtle, were gentle, compassionate human beings. It had been a welcome surprise to Rachel when she realised the two sisters had taken Hannah to their hearts.

"You're right about me not being a good milkmaid," said Rachel, standing up and dusting the straw from her clothing before lifting the pail. "But we've enough milk for ourselves and Jamie can get on with the rest of the milking when he gets back."

"No, no, no!" protested Ishbel. "Remember, I came out a good hour ago to tell you that a force nine gale was forecast for this afternoon."

"So?" queried Rachel, who was still unused to the emphatic and precise speech of the islanders.

"Well, our fishing fleet, who will have heard the radio issue the same storm forecast, will by now have run for shelter in case the gale reaches force ten." Ishbel crossed herself before continuing, "And our Jamie, God bless him, will now be safely in Mallaig eating the fish and chips."

"Eating fish and chips in Mallaig?" Rachel gasped incredulously, wondering why he hadn't simply made straight for home on this small isolated island of Herrig out in the Atlantic just west of Uist.

"Oh yes, indeed, the best fish and chips on the west coast are to be had from the chip shop on the pier at Mallaig."

By now the two women had left the byre and were advancing towards the house. As Rachel looked over the island and peered beyond into the far Atlantic, she was amazed to see that the horizon was dominated by what seemed to be a massive wall of water approaching from the west.

"What in the name of heaven is that?" she asked, setting down the pail and pointing.

"That!" cried Ishbel in horror, "That is . . . oh, Holy Mary, Mother of God, help us in our hour of need," she fervently cried out while crossing herself.

"Help *us*?"

"Oh aye, we will surely need Our Lady's help, right enough! That monster out there will grow and grow and as it gathers momentum it will destroy all that lies in its path when it runs ashore."

"So you've seen this before?"

"Not often. In fact, just the three times. Once was back in 1900. Now what was the date? Aye, I mind now. It was December the fifteenth in that year, when there was another such great tidal wave. My father and I prayed for help just where we are standing now and the Good Lord steered it away to the north." She paused before adding, "Aye, but it ran ashore on Flannan Isle and the three poor lighthouse keepers there were swallowed up and never seen again."

"So when it reaches here it will be a force *ten* then?"

"No."

Rachel swallowed hard. "So it will be staying at force nine?"

"Maybe aye; maybe no," responded Ishbel. "That could have been what might have happened right enough. But see yonder, how the new moon looks as if it is lying on its back and how the wind is being challenged by our opposing tide."

"Yes, I see. But what does that mean?"

Ishbel pursed her lips and shook her head before answering, "That means the wave is heading straight for us and we can look forward to at least a force eleven chasing it."

"A hurricane!" shrieked Rachel.

"Aye, it's hurrying, right enough. See how it's galloping towards us."

As Rachel watched the momentous wave hurtle towards them she found it difficult to stem her increasing sense of panic. "Is that what you came to the byre to tell me?"

"No," replied Ishbel, "I didn't see the danger until right now. I came to tell you that I think ..." Ishbel hesitated before going on, "I could be wrong – but I think that Hannah has now commenced her labour."

"Begun her labour!" yelled Rachel. "But didn't you tell me the District Nurse had gone over to South Uist this morning?"

"Aye," said Ishbel gravely. "And there is no way she'll allow herself to be blown back here tonight by that monster."

"You mean the two of us might have to deliver the baby by ourselves?"

"Of course. And that will not be a problem. It will just be like assisting the ewes with the lambing."

Rachel shook her head in despair. Would there be any point, she wondered, in reminding Ishbel that she only knew how to cook a lamb – not *deliver* one?

She went and lifted the pail again and, trudging towards the croft house, she could foresee how badly it could all end up.

"Right," she told herself. "Pull yourself together, Rachel, my girl. What problems could there be? Well, no running water in the house is the first of these. There's a water pipe, but that's at the bottom of the hill and out of reach until the blasted gale dies down. Some things are essential," she argued. "Now what are they? Tilley lamps, for a start; and the Aga stove – we've got both these things – and a chemical toilet. But that's down in the byre. Finally, and most importantly, we've no doctor or nurse – so what do we do? Easy! It was Hannah who decided not to go into labour on her due date, so Hannah must just decide to put it off a little longer – like till tomorrow when help and water will be at hand."

By the time she reached the living room, Rachel was feeling almost optimistic; but the sight of Hannah hanging on to the back of a chair and moaning loudly roused all her anxieties again.

"Oh, Mum," groaned Hannah, "whatever are we going to do?"

Rachel swallowed hard. This was a situation she had never envisaged for Hannah. She'd always been convinced that Hannah, the first-born and brightest of her five children, would be a rising star and would end up Head Matron at the Royal Infirmary. But the instant Hannah had passed her final nursing exams and emerged as a fully qualified Staff Nurse, she had shocked everyone be declaring how she'd met a fisherman, and was going to marry him. Then the two of them would live romantically on a remote island in the Outer Hebrides. Rachel could still feel the rage that had engulfed her when she thought of all that wasted education – education that seemed to be of no use in this island culture where Hannah was thought at first to be plain stupid and then accepted as simply ill-prepared for real life. Jamie's aunts just couldn't believe that this highly intelligent young woman couldn't milk a cow, cut peat, gather seaweed, gut fish or plant potatoes – not to mention being unable to help ewes with their lambing or round up ponies. And now here they were today, marooned on this small island of Herrig, with Hannah apparently deciding it was the proper time to give birth.

A deep intake of breath from her daughter quickly reminded Rachel that, apart from everything else, Hannah's husband was stuck in Mallaig eating fish and chips and that she, Rachel Campbell, was all that stood between Hannah and disaster.

"Well," Rachel at length replied, turning to face Ishbel and Myrtle who were both seated quite calmly by the peat fire and were engaged in nursing young Morag between them. "How long do you think this storm will last?"

"Ah, to be truthful, you never can tell. But listen – it is quite fierce right now, so it could well blow itself out in three or four hours," replied Myrtle.

Rachel looked at the ceiling as she listened to the howling and shrieking of the wind. So ferocious was it that she began to wonder if the house, perched on the island's little hilltop, would still be standing in the next ten minutes. And, as if that wasn't bad enough, she accepted that there was no way anyone from the house could go out to seek for help. They would just have to manage. Then she thought of her own birth labours and how they had always been prolonged and hard – but that surely was the answer! Quickly, she turned to Hannah. "Look, girl. All you have to do is to drag your labour out. What I mean is, hold on for . . . for *at least* another five hours. Then we'll be able get you all the help you need."

Hannah looked aghast. "Hang on, Mum? Don't you realise it's a baby I'm having – not a tooth extracted!" Rachel was about to argue when there was a loud gurgling sound and Hannah screamed, "It's my waters – they've broken."

"So I see," remarked Rachel coolly, wondering what else she could possibly say. Then she saw that Hannah was trying to push. "Look Hannah," she instructed. "Take deep breaths. Cross your legs tightly. Pull in your stomach. Do anything but . . . please *don't* push."

"But I just have to! Oh, Mum. Come on, help me upstairs to bed."

That was indeed all that Rachel could do. Reluctantly, she accepted that the ferocity of the storm had beaten her and that midwifery was a skill she would just have to learn fast.

Hannah's labour was short, much too short for Rachel's liking, but even though it had all been very embarrassing and difficult for Rachel, who was always ultra-modest, it really had been remarkably trouble-free. And thanks to both mother and daughter laying aside their mutual self-consciousness, a big baby boy had been safely born.

Now, with the morning sunshine pouring in through the window and the wind having abated to a gentle breeze, Hannah was sitting up in bed coaxing the little boy to suckle while dainty little Morag lay tucked in beside her mother. Without looking directly at Rachel, Hannah said, "Thank you, Mum. I just don't know how I'd have managed to deliver him without your help."

"Aye well, believe me, it was more than the wind that wanted to howl last night."

Hannah now turned to face her mother. "You were scared?"

"Positively terrified!"

"Well, I never would have believed that. In fact, once you got into your stride I felt I was a little girl again. Sure, there were some problems, but I was blessed with a mother who could sort them all out."

Rachel stopped gathering up the washing and gazed pensively around the impoverished room before speaking. "Aye, but most of the time the only problems we had were the kind that a fiver could have put right. And know something, Hannah? If all you ever have to worry you in this world is finding a fiver, then count yourself lucky."

There was a lengthy pause before Hannah said quietly, "I know life here on Herrig wouldn't be for you, Mum. But I've grown to love it dearly. True, we've no modern facilities like electricity and water from the tap – but they're coming."

"When?"

"As soon as possible." Hannah paused before blurting out: "Mrs Cummings at the foot of the hill was telling me, only last week, that the electricity could be here as soon as 1959." Hannah could plainly see that Rachel was unimpressed by the news about the island's electricity coming in five years' time. Rubbing her hand gently over her son's cheek to encourage him to suck, she went on, "But that's all by the by. What's important is the quality of life I find here. The pace suits me – the contentment, and the comfort of my faith. I'm so very grateful for all of that. But most off all I love my husband and my wonderful children; and I'd rather give them a better quality of life here on this beautiful island without running water than live in a cold palace with a flushing lavatory."

Rachel accepted that there would be no use in trying to point out to Hannah that back in 1939 a flushing lavatory for their exclusive use had been something she herself had fought for, tooth and nail. Hadn't she taken on the whole of the Edinburgh Corporation? Didn't Hannah realise just what her mother had forced herself to do to get them out of the slum that was Admiralty Street (the same Admiralty Street that the bulldozers were now rightly pounding to dust) and get them resettled in Learig Close. She could still feel the thrill she'd experienced when Johnny and she had stood in the bathroom while she pulled the chain to flush the lavatory. That simple action symbolised how she had won a better life for her children. The days were finally over when the communal lavatory seat had to be disinfected before she would allow her offspring to sit on it.

"But I love you too, Mum, and I'm so grateful for all you've done for me."

Rachel turned to smile at that remark but the smile froze on her face when Hannah continued, "And now, being the mother of two, I realise how hard it must have been for you to come all the way here to help me out at the very time that Sam was coming home for the first time in eighteen months, and you wouldn't be there to welcome him."

Why, oh why, wondered Rachel with a pang of guilt, did this lassie have to remind her that Sam, her own Sam, would now be at home, feeling yet again that Hannah's needs were of greater importance than his? And when she did eventually get home, would he accept her explanation that she knew he was far more able to look after himself than Hannah was? Well, she conceded, that had been her firm belief until placid Hannah had just explained, so quietly yet so emphatically, what her priorities were – and how and where she meant to spend her life.

3
POLICE PRIORITIES

Stepping into the driveway of the Police Training School at Whitburn, Sam was confronted by row upon row of Nissen huts. The sight made him pull up so sharply that his suitcase tumbled to the ground. He had hoped that being accepted for his police training would manage to divert his mind from the horrors of Korea – but this old army training camp, for all that it was now serving a new purpose, immediately brought back the nightmares.

Sam was still standing rigid when the fellow who had followed him off the bus asked half-jokingly, "Taking cold feet?"

"Naw," blustered Sam, facing round to the man. "Ye were on the bus from Edinburgh like me, but that's no a Lothian accent ye have."

"It's Inverness I come from. And the name's Dougal McDonald," the chap replied, laying down his case and offering Sam his hand.

"Sam Campbell," Sam responded, shaking the out-stretched hand vigorously and taking an instant liking to this Highlander.

Picking up their cases, the pair made their way to the reception area where they were met by the duty officer, Inspector Smith, who showed them to a dormitory and advised them to choose a bed from the six empty berths out of the twelve available. He added that once they were settled in they should join the Commandant and other tutors in the main hall.

"Ah well," began Sam as the inspector closed the door on them. "At least I'll have a guid sleep the nicht. A bed all to myself again – the sheer luxury o it."

"You don't have a bed to yourself at home?"

"Naw. I share wi ma wee brother. Well, he *was* wee when I left to do my National Service, but in the space o twa years he seems to have sprouted to six feet and his size seven feet are now tens that kick the hell out o me the hale night long."

Dougal laughed. "And here was me thinking that I missed out on being a lonely-only."

By the time Sam and Dougal reached the main hall, the Commandant was already in full flight. "Now!" He paused momentarily to fix his gaze directly on Sam and Dougal. "Gentlemen, do take a seat while I recap . . . As I was saying, your instructors in all those subjects where you must become proficient are very highly experienced in their respective fields." He halted again and gestured towards the five tutors who were seated at his side. "Each one of these gentlemen will also act as a personal mentor for six of you out of our thirty new recruits. Now, when you leave here I wish you to go directly to Classroom C and spend some time writing about what you have done so far in your lives. Just a brief summary of your home-life, your schooling, your work experience and what sports you have taken part in."

Once in the classroom, Sam sat down at a desk, but instead of beginning to write he simply sat staring into space. He just couldn't see what good might come from describing what his childhood had been like. How do you explain that your Dad had thought so little of you and your siblings that he'd done a runner? And how his callous desertion meant you'd had to live by your wits. Sam finally decided that he wouldn't lie – but would couch Johnny's desertion in ambiguity. So, lifting up his pen, he simply wrote down that his mother had raised him and the rest of his family after his father's unexpected departure! With the Johnny problem out of the way he then confidently went on to write about everything else that had happened during his life – leaving to the last his love of football and his prowess in that sport.

Once they had both finished writing about themselves, Dougal and Sam made their way out into the corridor. Here they familiarised themselves with the notice board, which they had been counselled to check on a daily basis, as any individual instructions would be posted there. Nothing of any particular interest appeared for either of them until the Wednesday, when a neatly-typed instruction read: "PC 10 of Edinburgh City Police D Division should go, equipped with his football gear, to the entrance door of the School at 13.00 hours today. He will then be given transport to Edinburgh to take part in the mid-week Amateur League football match between Edinburgh City Police and RAF Turnhouse."

Sam at once sought out his mentor, Inspector Smith. "Sir," he began, "that football thing this afternoon – why me?"

"Look, Sam, you want to get on in your job, don't you?"

Sam nodded.

"Then just follow instructions."

"Okay, but how did they find out about me?"

The inspector was reluctant to answer that question, but even after three days of knowing Sam he realised he would have to explain. "Sandy Brown is manager of the Edinburgh Police football team and wants the very best players. So every intake day he phones up to ask if there are any decent footballers among the Edinburgh City recruits. Once he'd learned your name, he contacted Leith and . . . So just you be waiting outside to be picked up, eh?"

Obeying instructions, Sam had been standing in the driveway for a full fifteen minutes waiting to be picked up when a sleek black Jaguar unexpectedly swept in. Thinking that this mode of transport couldn't possibly be for him, he drew back as the car came smoothly to a halt. The driver then jumped out and asked, "You PC 10 Leith Division?"

"That's me," said Sam.

"Then jump in, back or front – suit yourself – but hold on to your hat. We've got only forty minutes to get you to Turnhouse."

Without a word, Sam opened the front door and slid inside. The car was the last word in luxury. Large, leather-upholstered seat facing an opulent instrument panel set in a walnut fascia that Sam just couldn't resist running his fingers over.

"Never been in a Jag then?" the driver asked.

"In a Jag? Never been in a car. Where I come from, the only two cars that were ever in the street were the doctor's and the sheriff officer's."

"So you don't drive?" Sam shook his head. "Never mind. All you have to do is do what I did and get eight lessons from the BSM. Then the police will put you through their test and you could end up like me in the Traffic Department driving all the VIPs about."

Sam smiled. "Well, to be truthful, I *can* drive a wee bit."

"You can?"

"Aye, ye see I did have a wee shot at driving an American tank in Korea."

The driver laughed.

Sam joined in. "Aye, right enough, I don't think that a Sherman would count. But thanks for the advice about the lessons. Being able to drive would really suit me, so it would."

Half an hour later and with a friendship already forged, they pulled in at Turnhouse RAF base camp and Sam jumped out.

"I'll pick you up at five sharp for the drive back," the driver called out as Sam raced towards the reception gate where he was immediately directed to the Police Team's dressing room. There he found that the team were already outside limbering up and that only one man remained in the room.

"I'm PC 10 Leith Division and I play centre-half," Sam announced, already feeling rather puffed up with his own importance.

"And I'm PC 60 C Division, team secretary for the Edinburgh City Police Football Team – and you're playing inside-left."

Sam shrugged stoically.

From the very outset Sam fitted in well with the team and never missed an opportunity. Twice he put the ball into the back of the net. And, with many of the RAF team being National Service boys who were already signed-up professional footballers, the final score of six goals apiece was a commendable result for the Police Team.

The Jaguar had just arrived to pick Sam up when he was approached by Sandy Brown, the team manager, who congratulated him on his performance. Sam, however, was now feeling even cockier and couldn't resist saying, "See that centre-half ye played the day? Is that his usual position?"

Sandy sucked at his upper lip before replying, "Had a bad game the day, he did. But listen, sonny boy, we all have our off-days – even a swollen-headed young ace like you could end up playing as if you'd never kicked a ball afore."

Sam offered a reluctant nod of agreement.

"Now, off ye go and we'll see you next week for the game against Glasgow City. And, believe me, the Glasgow Police field a no mean team."

Shaking his head, Sam demurred, "But I can't go to Glasgow. I'm at the Training School."

"Forget the school. You just follow orders: next week you'll be required to play at Glasgow."

Sam wanted to argue that, although he loved playing football and knew he was good at it, his police career was very important to him – but the sound of the Jaguar horn had him scampering off.

The following week, on a dreadful ash pitch, the like of which Sam had never played on before, the Edinburgh team won by three goals to one. This time Sam didn't directly score any of the goals, but he did prove himself to be an excellent team player by setting up two of the goals for his team-mates to score.

It was on the bus back to Whitburn that Sam found Sandy had omitted to say just how important the Glasgow game was. By beating the Glaswegians, Edinburgh was now the only Scottish representative in the quarterfinals of the British Police Cup! Consequently, whenever Sam was away playing football, his friend Dougal was ordered to copy out all the lecture notes for Sam and it was Dougal who also had to tutor Sam on Police Procedure.

4
SILVER SERVICE

Back at last from her time on Herrig, Rachel arrived at the door of 16 Learig Close and smiled when she saw the key in the lock. That was just what she wanted – someone at home to greet her. However, when she unlocked the door and stepped into the living room, a distinct chill seemed to settle upon her and she gave an involuntary shiver – due more, she thought, to disgust at the sight of last night's ashes lying lifeless in the grate than to her annoyance at the general air of neglect in her home.

"Anyone home?" she called out.

The door from the bathroom creaked open and Alice emerged, her hair swathed in a towel, "Oh, it's you, Mum. We thought it was about time you came home."

"That so?" replied Rachel, picking up some clothes from a chair so that she could sit down. "Then why is this house looking like a midden?"

Alice looked critically round the room. "It's Carrie's fault. It was her turn to get things tidied up."

Rachel shook her head emphatically. "Carrie's turn? D'you mean to tell me you're prepared to sit in the cold simply because Carrie's not here to clean out the fire and reset it?"

Alice silently removed the towel from her hair, lifted a comb from the mantelpiece and started to drag it through her locks.

"And talking of Carrie, where the devil, is she? After all, she finishes at five. It's now gone six o'clock and she should have the tea on the table."

Alice sniggered. "Mum, you're not going to believe this but Carrie's away serving at a banquet in the *posh* Caledonian Hotel."

"She's what? But what on earth does Carrie know about silver service?"

"Not a blooming thing – but as soon as her pal down in the Roperie told her she would get paid twelve and six for the night's work she just had to give it a go."

Just then the door opened and Rachel jumped to her feet crying, "Sam! Oh, Sam!"

"Wrong, Mum. It's only me," Paul half sang to his mother.

"But where's Sam?" Rachel's hand flew to her mouth. "Don't tell me he's had a relapse of that flaming malaria."

"Naw," replied Paul. "But if you wanted to see him you should have got home on Sunday."

"Sunday? So where is he now then?"

"At the Police Training School – if you stick around till Friday he'll be home for the weekend."

Rachel bristled. Why did her other children so resent her going off to help Hannah? Couldn't they appreciate that Hannah's needs were so much greater than theirs? Without uttering another word she took off her coat and knelt down to begin cleaning out the fire. What she really wanted to do was to sort Alice and Paul out – but was this the time to challenge them about their disrespect? A loud knock at the outside door settled the matter. Turning, she signalled to Paul with a curt toss of her head that he should answer the summons.

"Oh, Mum," he shouted back, "it's a telegram boy!"

Slowly Rachel rose off her knees. "Oh, no! Oh no, no, no!" she exclaimed.

The sheer opulence of the Caledonian hotel held Carrie mesmerised. When she had followed her friend, Gertie, into the dining room she felt as though she'd been invited into the ball at the start of *Gone With the Wind*. It wasn't just the sheer beauty of the velvet curtains, the deep pile of the carpets, or the tables set with crisp white linen and real silver cutlery that held her spellbound. No, it was the open doors at the bottom of the room that led out into the guests' waiting-area, where a pianist sat, resplendent in evening dress, playing heart-wrenching romantic music at the Steinway. The music quickened all of Carrie's senses. Gazing at those diamond-encrusted ladies in their flowing evening gowns beside their handsomely-kilted escorts, she wondered why the world should be so ill-divided.

A loud whisper from Gertie halted Carrie's day-dreaming. "What was that you said?" she asked, thinking that maybe she should get out quick.

"Just that Paddy Fowler . . ."

"Paddy *who*?"

"The Head Waiter – him that's still talking."

"Oh, I see," Carrie mumbled, as Paddy reiterated how regrettable it was that, due to an outbreak of sickness and diarrhoea, nearly all of the permanent staff were off sick, which meant that he was virtually dependent on the temporary hired staff. It also meant that instead of two waiting staff per station there would only be one!

The news shook Carrie. She had been positively assured by Gertie that she would simply be assisting a fully-trained waiter who would keep her right. Whatever was she to do now? True, she could serve up meals no bother – but in her mother's house everyone had an equal share of everything and if they didn't feel like eating something they just passed it over to someone who did. Well, that was what she would do here – just dish up as she would do at home.

She was sure the first course would be no problem. All she had to do was to ladle the cock-a-leekie from the tureen into the soup plates. Unfortunately, she didn't always make certain, as Gertie had told her beforehand, that there was to be one prune placed in every plate. Her other blunder (which some of the guests regarded as a personal slight) was to serve the men first! Carrie was astonished to discover that the men were supposed to be served last. All her life she had been told that the breadwinners must come first at mealtimes.

When it came to the main course, Carrie decided it could be dished up at the sideboard – but Dai Morgan, the deputy Head Waiter, now designated to keep an eye on her, snapped, "No! No! No! All silver service must be at the table, beginning with the ladies. Is that quite clear?" Carrie meekly assented and did succeed in placing a sirloin steak accompanied by a fondant potato on each plate; but the trouble started when it came to the petits pois. She tried to scoop up the dancing peas with a fork and spoon but they would keep slipping off. That mightn't have mattered so much if the lady she was serving hadn't leant over to whisper to the gentleman sitting on her right, leading to Carrie's hand being bumped. Control of both serving dish and spoon was thereupon completely lost – the peas cascading down the lady's bare back before finally burying themselves in the folds of her royal-blue evening gown.

The ensuing furore caused one gentleman at the top table to look round and Carrie was amazed to find herself being smiled at by a real and well-known Scottish Duke. Her eyes travelled along the table and saw that the lady on his left, the most beautiful and most elegant person she had ever seen, had her napkin pressed to her mouth in a vain effort to stem her laughter. Dai Morgan, however, was not laughing. Racing to the aid of the distraught lady, he ushered her from the room and summoned a chambermaid to repair the damage.

From the very start Carrie knew the sweet course would be a disaster. Why couldn't they have served up clootie dumpling or tinned pears with Carnation milk? No, it had to be flaming Baked Alaska resting upon a heavy silver platter. In spite of this, Carrie did manage successfully to serve two ladies but when she tried to persuade the meringue and ice-cream to leave the spoon and land neatly on the third plate it just wouldn't budge. Three times she tried to coax it off before lifting the spoon up high in desperation and giving it a tremendous whack. Instead of landing on the lady's plate, the Baked Alaska sailed backwards and with a loud plop deposited itself on the Duke's balding head. Being the gentleman he was, he made no fuss but continued to converse jovially with his fellow guests before lifting his napkin to wipe away the melting ice-cream. Already it had trickled into his eyes, down his nose and on to his upper lip. Unperturbed, he stuck out his tongue and licked it away.

Unfortunately, Dai Morgan lacked the Duke's fine breeding and Carrie found herself being verbally assaulted as he dragged her ignominiously from the dining room and out into the kitchen area.

"Out of here you go. Right now!" he screamed, wheeling about to return to the dining room.

"I'm going," retorted Carrie. "But I want my wages first."

Dai turned back. "You want paid for that fiasco? Don't you realise, woman, what you've done and who you have done it to?"

Carrie tossed her head assertively. "I still want my twelve and six or . . ." She paused dramatically before offering the ultimate threat: "Or else I go right back in there and serve the coffees!"

Dai spluttered with rage, dipped into his pocket, brought out a wad of notes, peeled off a ten-shilling note and thrust it into Carrie's outstretched hand. "That's it. Now bloody well go." Then, firmly pasting his well-practised smile back on his face, he fled back into the dining room.

Carrie watched him disappear before realising she had no idea how to get out of the hotel but, retrieving her coat, she calmly wandered around until she found a door that brought her into the foyer where the pianist was still playing.

Well, she decided, as she gazed about the palatial room, one day I'll sit in this room on one of these chairs and listen to such wonderful music while someone comes to serve me. She was quite certain that some day her dream would come true. A playful wink from the musician confirmed that prediction.

It was after nine before Carrie got home. She had meant to take a bus but being already half a crown down on the night she felt prudence rather than extravagance was now required.

Entering the family home, she smiled. Rachel was seated pensively by the glowing fire with a cup of tea in one hand and a half-slice of toast in the other. "Oh Mum, thank goodness you're safely back home from Herrig."

Rachel looked up and gave the hint of a smile.

"How's Hannah?" spluttered Carrie. "I mean, what did she have?"

"A boy. Going to call him Fergus, I think."

"Isn't she lucky? So that'll be her family complete already."

Rachel made no response to that. Everybody else might think that Hannah would now call a halt to her family but Rachel knew her eldest daughter better. Hannah would go on and on having children. Oh yes, a report last week had said the greatest problem for the Outer Hebrides was a falling population – but that was a problem Hannah would take great pleasure in resolving.

"Anything to eat?" asked Carrie, breaking sharply into Rachel's thoughts.

"Eat? Well, the shops were closed by the time I got back. And all I found in the cupboard were two eggs, a tin of beans and some potatoes. So I cooked egg, chips and beans for Paul and Alice, then made a plate of porridge for myself. Here," Rachel continued, "you can have the last bit of toast though."

Carrie sniffed as she took the toast and started to devour it. "I wouldn't want to take it, Mum, but I really am starving."

"Didn't you get some of the banquet leftovers?"

"I came away before the divvy-up."

"Why?"

"I was sacked."

"Sacked?"

"Aye. Honestly, all that carry-on just to dish up a meal. And it wasn't my fault. I should have only been putting plates out and picking them up – not trying to scoop up silly wee peas with a spoon and fork!"

Rachel shook her head. "Well, wee peas are the least of your worries. Look . . ." and she pointed to the telegram that was propped up on the mantelpiece.

Carrie jumped up, grabbed the telegram and tore it open. Her jaw dropped and tears sprang to her eyes.

"Will's been killed?" croaked Rachel, struggling to keep her alarm in check.

Carrie shook her head. "No. Worse than that!"

"Worse?"

"Aye. He'll be home in six weeks. And I'm instructed to book the Co-op's Kintore Rooms in Queen Street for our wedding reception at the beginning of February."

"But isn't that exactly what you want?"

"Course I do. But Mum, I told you about Will's mother. She wants to invite *fifty* folk to the wedding. And I would get such a red face if we didn't invite fifty."

"Okay, but what's the real problem?"

"Where the devil are we going to find the money for a hundred people to have steak pie and trifle in the Kintore Rooms when they charge at least two and sixpence a head? And if that's not bad enough, Will thinks we should have sandwiches and sausage rolls later on . . ." Carrie sniffed loudly before bawling, "at another one and tuppence a head. And I'm certain his mother will get the dividend from it all because it's *her* store number it's to go on!"

"See what you mean, Carrie. But you know I'm chipping in all I can. The two-tier wedding cake is costing me six pounds – mind you, that does include four favours. And the material and making up of the dresses for you and Alice, well, wonder if I should try robbing a bank?"

5

WEDDING PLANS AND PIMPERNEL PETE

Rachel smiled at Sam who had just entered the kitchen. "Sleep well?"

"No I didnae!" he retorted. "Ye ken fine Paul needs the hale o that bed for himself."

Rachel avoided the topic. "Fancy a bacon roll?"

"Aye. But dinnae change the subject." Mellowing his tone, Sam wheedled, "Look, Mum, I can't go on spending every night being kicked black and blue."

Mother and son eyed each other. Both were remembering when the single bed had been bought – and why! At thirteen, Sam had been masturbating in the bathroom just as his mother climbed up to clean the outside of the bathroom window. Looking through the clear upper pane Rachel had been horror-stricken to see her precious, innocent boy abusing himself in such a way. So great was her distress that she'd fallen off the ladder; but once she'd picked herself up she had raced into the house and begun to thrash Sam with the carpet-beater. Paul's claim that Sam was only polishing his conkers had merely added to her fury. Once her anger was spent, Rachel had stipulated that from then on Sam was never to be allowed to sleep in the same room and bed as his mother and sisters. He and Paul, his younger brother, were henceforth to be banished to the empty room to sleep on a palliasse. One week later she'd purchased a single bed for her boys on the never-never. That bed had served the two boys perfectly well as wee laddies – but two energetic six-footers had different needs. Rachel admitted that. "Okay," she said, more to herself, "I know I promised to buy a bed-settee for Paul so you could have the room all to yourself, especially now you'll be working shifts but . . ." she heaved a deep sigh, "this blasted royal wedding of Carrie's is costing the earth."

Sam remained silent. He was still thinking back to why the single bed had been bought. How on earth, he wondered, had his mother, who had such an abnormal aversion to sex in all its forms – and that even included speaking about it – managed to give birth to five children? Debating the matter mentally, he concluded they couldn't have all been immaculate conceptions – or could they? Looking again at his prim mother he concluded that they really couldn't have been anything else!

Covertly taking out his bulging wallet, he declared, "Well, if a bed-settee is the only thing that stands between me and a guid night's sleep, I'll just have to buy yin myself."

Unable to hide her surprise and wondering how Sam's wallet had come to have so much inside it, Rachel waited for an explanation. None was forthcoming but Sam did finally ask, "Could we go down to Leith Provident and get it after breakfast?"

Rachel consented.

They had just begun to eat their bacon rolls when Carrie came into the kitchen and sat down beside them.

"Why d'you always have to have a face that could follow a funeral?" demanded Rachel.

"Oh Mum, see Will's mother? Know what she wants now?" Rachel shook her head.

"A piper at the church *and* at the reception!"

"And who's going to pay for all that carry-on?"

"I don't know," Carrie whispered before swallowing and adding, "but I think that with them paying for the band and the bar . . ."

"They're paying for the bar?" queried Sam.

"Aye," said Carrie. "Seems that at all Highland weddings the groom's parents pay for the bar – and it's free all night."

"They're putting on a free bar *all* night long?"

Carrie nodded.

"Never thought I'd say it," smirked Rachel, "but know something? I'm real blinking sorry that my father Gabby's dead. Even the Frasers couldn't afford what he could drink!"

Carrie didn't reply but picked up a bacon roll and groaned. The only thing that had gone right with the wedding arrangements this week was the tête-à-tête she'd had with her old school pal, Bernie. Bernie had been married to a Glasgow boy for a year now. She didn't come back home to visit very often as her mother kept declaring she had married beneath herself by getting hitched to a Glasgow lad. But Carrie knew that Mrs Flynn's dislike of her son-in-law was less to do with him being a Glaswegian and more to do with him being a Rangers' supporter!

Carrie and Bernie did write frequently to one other; but what Carrie had been desperate to ask Bernie about simply couldn't be committed to paper. Last weekend, though, Bernie had luckily turned up at her mother's. Carrie barely allowed time for her old pal to greet her parents before she was scampering over the newly-erected outdoor coal bunkers that now separated each of the four-in-a-block housing gardens. Racing to Mrs Flynn's front door she knocked impatiently.

Thankfully, it was Bernie who answered the summons. But she just couldn't understand why Carrie insisted that they should huddle on the bottom step of the freezing stair rather than sit inside by a louping fire. "Right, what's the problem?" Bernie demanded.

Carrie lost no time in explaining that it was the old one – sex. The very first time the topic had been raised was when Bernie and Carrie were thirteen. They'd been going round to the chip shop for a snack when Rachel, who always seemed to have a washing cloth in her hand when the subject was broached, began to clean the bunker top vigorously before calling out to her daughter, "Now, just you watch what you do, Missie, and don't bring any disgrace on this family!" Carrie had been bemused. What disgrace could a bag of chips bring even if you did put on too much muck sauce? It was another two years before Rachel plucked up courage to refer to the subject again. For the first time Bernie and Carrie were going up town to the Friday night dance at the Palais de Dance in Fountainbridge. "Carrie, you do know, don't you, that all men are only after the one thing?" Rachel stated bluntly.

Carrie stopped combing her hair and turned to face her mother but Rachel was now down on her knees vigorously attacking the hearth with a washing cloth. Why, wondered Carrie, did her mother never look at her when she was issuing such statements? It was then that Aunty Bella, who had called in for a blether with Rachel, agreed. "You're right there, Rachel. They dream about it nicht an day, so they do." This statement from Bella confused Carrie still further, especially when Bella went on to say, "And you, Carrie, having been brought up in the true Protestant faith, have a duty to make sure their dreams dinnae come true."

Later, when Carrie and her friend were going for the bus, Bernie spoke about how her mother had also advised Bernie that all men were only after one thing! The only difference was that, when Bernie's mother got to the bit where she warned her daughter about not allowing men's dreams to come true, it was because Bernie had been brought up in the only true faith – the Roman Catholic one. Bernie then suggested to Carrie that she should ask Sam what it was he dreamed of all the time. Carrie declined this suggestion, pointing out that Sam wouldn't divulge such information unless he was paid to do so.

The following Saturday, Sam was on his way out when Bernie ran up the path and waylaid him. "Sam," she said, "I'll give you three slugs from this bottle of sugarallie water and a penny-dainty if you'll tell me what you dream about aw day lang."

Sam took the dainty from Bernie, then grabbed the bottle and gulped down half its contents. Disgusted at his greed, Bernie grabbed the bottle back. "Right," she said firmly. "I'm waiting."

Wiping his mouth with the back of hand, Sam lifted both arms high in the air and shouted, "What do I dream aboot aw the time? Nothing mair than aboot the Hibees winning the Cup!"

Carrie's thoughts came back to the present. She just had to speak to Bernie. Swallowing hard, she looked about to make sure they couldn't be overheard before whispering, "Know how you've been married for over a year now?" Bernie nodded. "And you're no . . . Well, you're no, are you?"

"You mean I haven't got a bairn?"

"Aye."

"So?"

"How do you manage no to? Everybody else seems to get one nine months later or even earlier."

"Simple! I practise birth control."

43

Carrie sighed. "Good. Now, I don't want to start a family for five years. First I've got to get away from Will's mother, so I need a house and a bed."

"Then just you do what I do."

"I want to – but I don't know what it is that *you* do!"

Bernie shook her head. "Look, it's simple. When, you know what I mean – when it happens – and don't believe your mother that it's any bother, 'cause it's no bother at all – well, no for me anyway – you just jump straight out of the bed and stand your bare feet on the cold floor for five minutes and then swallow a big drink o water!"

"And that does it?"

"Aye, everything then just drops down or gets flushed away. Easy-peasy!"

Sam pushed back his chair. "C'mon, Mum, afore the money for the bed-settee ends up paying the piper."

Carrie snorted. "You can mock, Sam, but Will's mother is driving me cuckoo. And Mum, Mrs Fraser says I've not to worry about paying for the wedding with some of the house deposit I've saved up."

Rachel's face lit up. "She's going to give it to you?"

Carrie shook her head. Tears were brimming. "No, no. She says I've to live in Will's room, even when he goes back to sea!"

"Well, that would let you save more and we'd have a bit more room here."

Shooting up her head, Carrie replied vehemently, "No, no! I might have to sleep there when Will's at home, because that's the only place we can be together." She sniffed loudly before adding, "But when he goes back to sea again I'll be back *here* with all of you."

Engulfed with a warm feeling of achievement at having successfully completed his police training, Sam was now on his way to the structure that housed Leith Municipal Buildings and Council Chambers. He knew all about the history of the imposing edifice on the corner of Constitution Street and Charlotte Street because all through his childhood his mother had regaled him with tales about Leith. One of these, which she'd told him over and over, was about the Council Chambers having been a symbol of the independence and wealth that proud Leith once had. Amalgamation with Edinburgh, however, had put paid to Council meetings and magistrates' courts being held there, although the building was still used by the Leith Police who had been there ever since its erection in 1828.

Entering through the impressive portico, Sam was still unprepared for the grandeur that faced him. The main marble staircase with its highly polished wooden banisters gave credence, in his opinion, to his mother's claim that Leith once had been a thriving, affluent port and should have protected its standing by remaining quite independent of Edinburgh. He was still standing mesmerised by the sheer opulence of the architecture when Sergeant Duff walked in.

"So you like the look of the old place?" commented the sergeant.

"Just great."

"Well, sorry to drag you away, but we go this way to the rabbit warren," and he beckoned Sam to follow him.

Once arrived at the operations centre, Sam had to acknowledge it was quite an eye-opener. Rooms and cells just seemed to go off in all directions: here, there and everywhere. The sergeant ushered Sam into a small room and, seating himself behind a desk, motioned Sam to take the seat opposite.

"Now," began Sergeant Duff, "I'm going to double you up with an experienced officer who'll show you the ropes."

Sam gave a nod of approval.

The sergeant rubbed his chin, sniffed, blew out his lips and seemed to ponder deeply before continuing, "I think Pimpernel Pete will be just the boy to break you in."

"Why's he called Pimpernel?"

"Because he has a habit of regularly disappearing and no matter where we seek him he always stays elusive." The sergeant spoke more to himself now. "You know, I just don't know where he gets to. Must have a howff somewhere. I'll need to find it."

"So you really think *he* would be a good mentor for me?"

The sergeant grimaced. "Only other alternatives are the Olympic Torch and . . ."

"Olympic Torch?" asked Sam, wondering if everyone in the Leith Division had a nickname. Later on he found that, in fact, they did.

"Aye, he's called Olympic Torch because, if he can help it, he never goes out – especially if it's raining. And as for Misty, well . . . he's not *quite* as thick as fog but no bright enough to find his own way back at the end of his shift."

"So it's to be Pimpernel Pete then?"

"Aye, 'cause out of the three of them, he'll moan the least when you have to take time off for your football."

"Just disappear, will he?"

"Uh, huh." The sergeant looked Sam straight in the eye before adding, "But you're a bright enough lad and I'm counting on you to just pick up from him only what you need to learn."

From the very start there was a kind of chemistry between Sam and Pete. They seemed to understand each other and automatically covered the other's back. Sam would never forget the first time they walked 8 Beat together. Pete had asked Sam all about his family and it turned out he'd known Gabby, Sam's alcoholic grandfather. Couldn't remember how often he'd picked him up drunk and incapable off the broad pavement.

"And how did you deal with him?" asked Sam, who was aware that Gabby hadn't appeared in court all that often.

"Just flung him in a cell and let him sleep it off. Never saw the point of having him transferred to the central charge office," he confided. "Ye see, son, the court would just have fined him – money he either didn't have or needed so he could get blotto again."

Sam chuckled. That had been Gabby, right enough. Oh aye, Sam could never remember his grandfather ever being sober . . . or indeed washed. And what with the drink and him being a failed gambler, Gabby had been yet another financial drain on his daughter, Rachel.

By the time they had exhausted their mutual Gabby stories, the pair had reached the Craighall Road crossroads in Newhaven where Pete halted sharply and bundled Sam into the doorway of a tenement. Two speeding cars, approaching from different directions, held both officers' attention. A collision was inevitable and as they smashed into one another the bang reverberated like a clap of thunder. Sam was first to recover from the shock and immediately unbuttoned his top pocket to take out his notebook but found himself being restrained by Pete as he geared himself up to run to the scene.

"Steady, laddie. Steady. Don't be over-enthusiastic," cautioned Pete calmly. "Let's just take our time and assess the situation before we go charging in."

"But . . ."

"No buts. Just look."

Sam looked towards the two drivers who were now out of their cars and seemingly uninjured. Both were staring directly at Sam and Pete, clearly expecting them to intervene. But as the seconds ticked by they realised that no intervention was forthcoming; so names and address were exchanged before they climbed back into their respective cars and drove off.

"Now," said Pete, "you've just had your first lesson in time-management! Should we have got overzealous and involved, we'd have had to make out a whole VAR – that's a Vehicular Accident Report. And that would have curtailed my community policing at yon bar over there because I'd have had to charge them both with speeding or careless driving. And, sure as hell, they'd have taken umbrage; and neither would have had their documents on them and that would have meant two HORT1s."

Sam looked puzzled. "HORT1s?"

"A Home Office Road Traffic One, laddie! Another bureaucratic waste of our valuable time and a further delay to me quenching my thirst."

Pete could see that Sam thought his approach was misguided at the least so he decided to explain how corners should be cut as and when they could. "Look, Sam," he said. "Never take the public's initiative away. They like to sort things out for themselves and as long as there's no fisticuffs they should definitely be allowed to do so! Now, let's go over and see that there's no illegal drinking being done in Drouthie's." Pete nudged Sam and winked. "Well, that's after we've downed a pint."

What with the car crash and the barman's promptitude in pulling two pints as soon as they entered the bar, Sam felt quite unsettled. And although Pete quickly emptied both glasses when he discovered Sam was teetotal, his pupil was positively bewildered by the time they reached the boundary between B Division and Leith.

They were just approaching Victoria Park, which marks an invisible dividing line between the two Divisions, when they became aware of a bundle lying just inside the Leith sector. Pete was first to discover that the bundle was a dead tramp. Rolling him over, he ascertained that this was probably a sudden death with no suspicious circumstances – no suspicious circumstances, that is, so far as the actual death was concerned. However, Pete recognised the tramp and knew the body was that of Johnny Bundles who lived and drank in B Division. Leith had been anathema to Johnny ever since he'd been barred from the most notorious pub there – the Jungle. That slight had been too much for Johnny, an educated man who had long since forsaken life in the upper echelons of society for the freedom of the open road; and he had vowed never to patronise Leith again. And he had never broken that vow. So why was the old gent lying on their Leith patch? Pete looked at his watch and pronounced, "Nearly finishing time and if we ring this one in we'll be late getting off."

"So?"

"Well, Sam, that would mean you'd be short of your beauty sleep before your afternoon training session. Besides, this body has already been moved. Feel it – rigor mortis has set in; it's wet underneath him and the rain only came on half an hour ago. See that B Division? Honestly, you can't keep up with them! So let's play them at their own game and help me put Johnny back to where he wants to be."

Pete began to roll the body resolutely back into B Division's Drylaw area. Sam, however, couldn't bear not following correct police procedure.

"Okay," said Pete patiently. Don't help me move him. But you go round now to the box and call in that there's a dead body lying in the street at Victoria Park. Oh, and be sure to tell them that we have ascertained that life is extinct due to natural causes – until a post mortem tells us otherwise. But, most importantly, advise Sergeant Duff that, as the body is lying ten feet inside the Drylaw area, B Division officers should attend and arrange for an ambulance – and write the report!

Within three minutes of Sam ringing in, two Drylaw officers were on the scene. The younger of the pair exclaimed loudly: "See this? That body's been moved too far into our area. We only shifted it four feet to get it into Leith!"

6
HOUSING AFFAIRS

Seated at her kitchen table, Rachel felt a sense of contentment for the first time in weeks. The main reason for her
disquiet had been the spiralling cost of Carrie's wedding.
She wanted to do her best by Carrie, but Will's parents –
who apparently never had to wonder where the next meal
was coming from – were making such grandiose demands.
They'd even invited people from as far afield as Muir of
Ord, the Black Isle, and Sutherland – so a boiled ham sandwich, a treacle scone or a fairy cake in Rachel's kitchen certainly wasn't going to be adequate, was it? But here she was
today with one real plus from this fiasco – Hannah, her precious Hannah, along with her two children, had arrived to
attend the wedding in a week's time. This meant that tonight
Rachel would have all her children around her. She'd
already dished up the evening meal. Those who were at
home were now tucking into their mince, tatties and dough-
balls, while Sam and Carrie's helpings had been plated up
and were sitting over two pots of simmering water on the
stove.

Rachel chuckled to herself when she recalled the look
of horror on Hannah's face the moment she'd stepped off
the afternoon train – naturally she'd expected her mother
to meet her but not holding on to a pram borrowed from one
of the neighbours. "Oh, Mum," Hannah had exclaimed,
"surely you don't expect me to walk all the way to Learig
Close from Princes Street!"

"It's only a good stretch of the legs," Rachel had replied,
taking hold of Fergus and tucking him in at the top of the

pram. Turning to dainty Morag, she swung her up and deposited her at the bottom, snuggling a blanket around her. Then she looked down at the two suitcases that a helpful fellow-passenger had dumped on the platform for Hannah. "I suppose, right enough," she continued, pointing to the luggage, "you wouldn't manage to carry these all that way." Hannah shook her head. "Tell you what! You get the bus, Hannah, and I'll walk with the bairns."

As Rachel hurried past the Duke of Wellington's statue, she glanced up at the Register House clock and thought how lucky she was that she'd had more backbone than that old lady (another Rachel) who had waited there, day in and day out, year in and year out, hoping that the man who had promised to marry her would some day turn up between noon and three o'clock when the registry office was open. Without a word of recrimination, she would have slipped her arm through his and scurried off to the registrar's office in Queen Street where at long last they'd be married. "Register Rachel" the people of Edinburgh had called the old woman, though that wasn't her real name. No one knew what she was called because, from the very first day that she had turned up dressed in all her wedding finery to the day she had suddenly disappeared fifteen years later, she had never spoken to a soul. As the years went by, her clothes had become ever more worn and tattered, her skeletal fingers protruding through the frayed gloves. The bunch of artificial violets that were to be pinned on her wedding hat were by then colourless and bedraggled. Yet every day without fail she had arrived to hold her vigil – even when she was so crippled with arthritis that she had to bring a three-legged stool to sit on. What a pity, thought Rachel, that the poor soul hadn't been brought up in Leith or known Eugenie, her own suffragette mistress who so many years ago had instilled into Rachel the wisdom that no man was worth waiting fifteen minutes for — never mind fifteen years! Looking back at the Register House clock, Rachel shivered involuntarily. Yes, she had noticed last week that the blooming clock had stopped. Indeed, it remained exactly at noon – the appointed hour that Register Rachel had arranged to meet her lover!

By the time Rachel had stopped reminiscing, she was cheerfully pushing the pram along the garden footpaths at London Road. Inevitably her thoughts turned back to Carrie – another dreamer not all that unlike Register Rachel. Was it really only three weeks ago that Will had come home? Carrie's excitement had been bubbling over as she prepared to meet the Liverpool train he was on. "Mum," she'd exclaimed, "what if we don't recognise each other? I mean, how long do you think it will take for us to get to know each other again?"

Rachel could only chuckle at that. How on earth, she wondered, could anyone who kissed a photograph at least ten times a day forget what the person looked like? And as for getting to know each other again . . . well, it had only taken five seconds before Carrie had sprinted up the platform and flung herself into Will's outstretched arms. Ever since then Carrie, just like Register Rachel, had been living in that blissful state of romantic illusion where it all ends up happy ever after. Rachel laughed again to herself as she remembered eavesdropping while Carrie described to her sister Alice what she thought her first night of married life would be like. "I just *know*," Carrie had croaked in a whisper, "that it'll be exactly like it is in the films – with waves crashing on the shore and classical music reaching a crescendo while seabirds swoop, dive and cry out in ecstasy." Rachel had been tempted to interrupt and tell Carrie she was living in a fantasy world. And if she expected to hear an orchestral climax – well, she was in for a shock. The only sound would be . . . Rachel grimaced and her cheeks flamed: best not to go on. No, that memory of hers was to be closed forever.

The outside door opened and Carrie and Sam barged in together. "Wherever have you two been?" demanded their mother, rising to turn off the gas from under the pots before adding, more pleasantly, "But sit you both down." Lifting the covers from the plates, she scowled. "Well, these dough-boys were light and fluffy when you should have been here to eat them – but if you're hungry enough you maybe won't notice you could heel your boots with them now."

Before sitting down, Sam went over and hugged Hannah. "Just seeing you has cheered me up." Turning to little Morag, he laughed. "Well, are ye no just dandy? Perfection in miniature, is she no?"

Hannah, who was now being cuddled by Carrie, called out over her sister's shoulder, "And why should you be needing cheered up, Sam? You suit the uniform. Don't tell me the job doesn't suit you?"

They all turned to look at Sam, who was now vigorously attacking his meal. He stopped briefly to reply, "Och, I do like the job. Hate a day like this one though. A ten to six shift because I had to report to the court and the blinking lawyers had done a last-minute plea deal. That meant I wasn't needed as a witness. Total waste of resources, that is. But see, Mum, when I got back to the station – there'd been a murder in the Leith Links last night."

"So I hear. Some woman, they say, who'd been slashed real bad by an American sailor."

Sam gulped. "My first involvement with a murder – and it had to be . . ."

"You *knew* her?" asked Carrie.

"Not *her* – *him*! Och, what am I going to say to Chalky? It was his cousin from the Dumbiedykes – the transvestite. But ken something? His family loved him. They just adored him."

Rachel's hand flew to her mouth. "You're right there, Sam," she agreed. "And no mother should have to bury her own bairn."

Hannah was more philosophical. "Yes," she remarked, "he was just a harmless, mixed-up young lad who'd been born a he when all he ever wanted was to be was a she. And no way should anyone have butchered him for that."

Rachel nodded and turned again to Sam. "Did you see his Mum?"

"Naw. CID dealt with that – but they're a load of heartless scum. Honestly, they can't even spell the word compassion – never mind show any."

"So what was your involvement, Sam?" Hannah questioned.

"Me? Ah well, because I was back from court early I had to type up some witness statements."

"You mean you can type?"

"Aye, Carrie," Sam replied holding up his two index fingers and wiggling them. "You'd be surprised what I can do when I have to."

Next day Sam had arrived early to ring in at the start of his back shift at Beat 8 police box. The morning constable was pleased to see him and without saying a word, rang headquarters to report his own signing-off and Sam's return to duty. A few seconds later, Sam was surprised to be handed the phone by PC Paddy Flannigan, better known as "Shadow" because, being a keen amateur boxer, he took every opportunity to shadow-box – even in the confined space of a police box! "They want to talk to you – *personally*," said Shadow, ducking and diving with his head.

Reluctantly, Sam took the phone and was somewhat taken aback to be told he had to proceed immediately to Charlotte Street Headquarters.

"Had I no better bide here till the van arrives with the crime reports and then cadge a lift?" suggested Sam, sensibly enough.

"Look, laddie. With the bother your mate's in," the station clerk told him, "I think a long walk might be a better idea. You can spend the time getting your side of the story straightened out!"

Taking the clerk's advice, Sam meandered along to Granton Road by way of Goldenacre and then along Commercial Street before finally reaching Charlotte Street. There, he was sent immediately to see Inspector Johnstone, a fanatical Wee Free from the Western Isles, who not only abstained from alcohol but also demanded that everyone else did likewise. Sam noted that the inspector wasn't exactly foaming at the mouth – but his eyes were certainly dancing with rage. "Now, Police Constable Campbell, don't lie to me."

Sam was silent.

"Are you aware that your mentor, PC Capaldi, frequents liquor establishments and imbibes . . ." the inspector stopped abruptly and screwed up his face in disgust before spitting the words out "... imbibes alcoholic beverages whilst on duty?"

Sam took some time to consider his reply. He knew he had to satisfy the inspector, whose fingers were now drumming furiously on the desk. "Well, sir, I've had a good training from Pim . . . Peter Capaldi and, as he knows I'm strictly tee-total, he allows me to check out all the empty dwelling houses while he makes sure that the public houses are conducting their business in accordance with the law. And I can assure you I have never seen him the worse for drink."

"So you're saying you've never seen him drink on duty."

"No. What I'm saying is I've never witnessed him to be the worse of drink." This statement was absolutely true because Sam knew well that Pimpernel Pete could hold his liquor – in fact, Sam reckoned it was being tanked up that made him function as brilliantly as he did.

"And I suppose you're also going to tell me that you never witnessed the punch-up at seven o'clock last night between him and the Drylaw officers."

Sam shook his head.

"You mean you didn't attend at the scene of a two-car vehicular accident on the boundary line?"

"No, sir."

"And why didn't you?"

"Because I was at home, eating mince and tatties."

"You left your shift to go home and eat mince and tatties?" the inspector spluttered.

"No, sir."

"Are you trying to make a fool of me?"

"No, sir," replied Sam, who thought the inspector managed that for himself. "I was at home yesterday evening since I'd had to do a ten to six shift because of a court attendance."

The inspector leant back in his chair and rubbed his hand over his mouth. "Well, for your information, there was a vehicle accident, resulting in one damaged car on the Drylaw side of the road and the other crashing into a fence on our side of the road. The officers who attended, from both Divisions, began to argue as to whose responsibility it was and squared up to each other when they couldn't agree. Once the ambulance arrived, the two officers who had come off worst in the fisticuffs had to be taken to hospital for treatment. Complaints from several members of the public were directed straight to the Deputy Chief Constable, with the result that Constable Capaldi has been transferred forthwith to the home beat. Mind you, how the Deputy Chief Constable expects me to keep Capaldi out of the Bonds – not to mention the wilder hostelries at every ten yards – I simply don't know. And you, Sam, since the DCC doesn't want your future compromised, will also work on the home beats out of here."

"Very well, sir," Sam meekly responded, finding it hard to hide his relief that the Pimpernel had been dealt with so lightly. But then Pete and the Deputy had joined the force together and their wives were the best of friends!

Later, while Sam was checking certain empty dwelling houses off Restalrig Road, he found himself in Cornhill Terrace, a street of substantial stone-built terraced villas. The occupants were all what might be described as middle-class. No child in this street would attend the local Edinburgh Corporation schools. They would be enrolled instead at one of the many fee-paying establishments such as Leith and Trinity Academies or the Royal High. Their fathers would be professional white-collar workers while their mothers (in some cases at least) would employ a woman to do the scrubbing.

Strolling up the street, Sam noticed that the curtains were invariably drawn securely over the windows – unlike those in Elbe Street, down the road towards the docks, where the working-class folk were so weary sometimes that the very effort of pulling the blinds was beyond them. On his arrival at the next empty dwelling he was due to check, Sam noticed that the house was decidedly out of keeping with the rest of the street. The windows were filthy, the frames were in need of at least one coat of paint and the small front garden was completely overgrown with weeds. Sam stepped up to the front door, lifted the letterbox and shone his torch though. All he could see were dirty bare floorboards but as he took a breath he found himself inhaling a foul, musty, airless odour. Turning to get some fresh air, Sam became aware that the neighbour from upstairs was now standing in the pathway.

"Evening, sir," said Sam politely, touching his officer's cap in respect.

The man extended his hand. "Leech. Andrew Leech is the name."

"Has this house been vacant long?"

"Too long. The old couple, both well into their nineties, died nearly two years ago. They weren't able to do much in their last years. Place got run down. Now, no one wants to buy it."

"They don't?"

"No. A shame really, because this is a good address. And the property is solid – stone built in the early nineteen hundreds." The man sighed. "But nowadays people want just to move straight in and sit down."

Sam pondered before asking, "How much do these houses go for?"

Mr Leech swung his head from side to side, obviously thinking carefully before inviting Sam into his own upper-villa home.

Sam was impressed with the sweeping staircase that led up to a large, well-carpeted drawing room with an ornate marble fireplace, shuttered windows and velvet tie-backed drapes. Mrs Leech was relaxing on a high-backed chair with her embroidery in her lap. "The house underneath has the same space. Just needs a fair bit of renovation," explained Mr Leech.

From the drawing room the two men eventually made their way to the bedroom, living room, bathroom and kitchen. Sam remained impressed. So he should be – for the Leech family had both money and status. He was a retired bank manager and his wife was the only child of a Leith chandler.

"As I asked before, how much do you think the house downstairs would go for?"

"Thinking of buying it yourself?" Mr Leech waited for an answer from Sam but as none was forthcoming he continued. "They were asking for thirteen hundred but . . ."

Sam shook his head.

". . . I think if someone was to make an offer of, say, eleven hundred because of the deterioration it's suffering – well, I think the solicitors would advise their clients to accept."

"Who are the solicitors?"

Mr Leech beamed. "Shiels and Mackintosh, just up from your base in Queen Charlotte Street."

Sam smiled. He knew now that Mr Leech hadn't hailed originally from Leith. All Leithers used the old name, Charlotte Street. *Never* did they say the new name imposed on them by Edinburgh Corporation to distinguish it from their very posh and elegant Charlotte Street.

Sam couldn't believe his luck. He had wanted to get Will on his own to tell him about the Cornhill Terrace house – and there he was, strolling up the brae in front of him. Had he first told Carrie about the house, she would have insisted on viewing it, despite the fact there was no way that Will and she could afford it. And that would send her into a foul mood for a good day or two.

"Will," Sam called out, quickening his pace, "I want a word."

As he unfolded the story about finding this wreck of a house in Cornhill Terrace – which was just a four minute walk from Learig Close – Sam could tell that Will was interested.

"If only we could get settled on a house before I'm called back to sea." Will paused and scraped his toes over the ground. "Look, Sam, you do know, don't you, that Carrie and my Mum . . . aren't . . . well, they're not exactly at log-gerheads but they're not entirely . . ."

"Compatible?" suggested Sam.

Hunching his shoulders and nodding, Will went on, "Carrie doesn't know just how hard life can be."

Sam chuckled to himself. Did Will Fraser imagine life had been a cake-walk for the Campbells when they were young? Even now, Carrie was still holding down two jobs at once so that she could pay her way. They'd all been taught never to be a burden; and Sam knew they never would be – well, not to him anyway.

"My brother being killed in the Malta campaign," Will continued, "was the last straw for my Mum. She seemed to cope with losing my two sisters in the thirties to measles and flu – and then, out of the blue, I came along. She didn't want a baby at forty-five, and still finds it difficult to be demonstrative to me . . . but I suppose I filled a gap in her life."

"I see," murmured Sam, as this new light was shed on Will's mother. "I'll try and speak to Carrie about giving your Mum more slack. But it's just that my sister imagines your Mum thinks a lot more of your cousins than she does of you. That hacks Carrie off for sure. Now, about this house?"

"D'you think we could sneak a look at it?"

"Your wish is my command," laughed Sam, giving an exaggerated bow.

Sam wiped his feet vigorously on the oversized doormat before opening the large half-glazed door of the solicitors' office. He wondered if either Mr Shiels or Mr Mackintosh was still practising. And he couldn't make up his mind if it was better to appear to be in the know or just to ask the receptionist for details of the house. He had decided to chance his luck – until he entered the reception area and was confronted by a face he knew: it was elegant Emma Stuart, whose long dark hair complemented an oval face that appeared bejewelled by her sapphire-blue eyes and ruby-red lips.

"How may I help you?" asked Emma, rising and offering Sam her hand.

"We-ell," spluttered Sam, thinking his dialect would sound alien to someone who had obviously been given elocution lessons. "Ye just might. Wondering, I was, if maybe I could get the keys to 105 Cornhill Terrace to have a butcher's at it."

"Butcher's?"

"Butcher's hook. A wee look-see."

Emma smiled. "Thinking of buying a house, are you?"

"Naw. Naw. No me. I'm a bachelor gay. But my twin sister's getting hitched next week and it's her that's needing a roof over her head."

Looking towards a glass key cabinet on the wall, Emma pursed her lips. "I'm sure it won't cause a problem to let you have the keys. But . . ."

"It wouldn't be a risk for ye. I'm in the polis down the road there."

Emma smiled. "Yes, I know you are. I saw you last week after my father insisted I should make myself useful by coming into the office here to help out."

"Ye're just helping out?"

"Yes. Daddy is the senior partner . . . and, as you can see, all the support staff are absent."

Sam looked around at the three unoccupied desks while he waited for a further explanation.

"It's that bad influenza epidemic doing the rounds," divulged Emma as she unlocked the cupboard, selected the keys to 105 and handed them to Sam. "My stint in here is finished tomorrow afternoon so I *must* have the keys back by then."

Accepting the keys, Sam winked before saying, "No problem. And, lassie, don't you fret – discretion is our byword. And thank you."

Extending her hand again and grinning, Emma replied, "No. Thank *you*. You've cheered up my day!"

The looking-over of 105 Cornhill Terrace was not so much a discreet viewing for the interested parties. It was more like a clan gathering for which all tickets had been sold.

Rachel was the first to speak. "Solid enough house. Just needs . . . And there's a nice wee back garden for your washing. So important to be able to hang out your washing."

Carrie sighed. That was her mother all over. Everything was just dandy if only you could get your washing hung out to dry. Her mother had even suggested recently that Mrs Anderson in the next stair to her in Learig Close would be canonised when she died simply for putting out such beautiful washings. Carrie had told her mother yet again that she wasn't fussed about doing beautiful washings – to which Rachel had replied that she had always known Carrie was lacking in ambition!

Breaking into Carrie's thoughts, Will's pipe-smoking father softly suggested, "It's the *potential* you have to look at."

Carrie beamed him a smile of agreement. He was such a canny highland gentleman: a retired police officer who spoke with a soft engaging lilt.

"You'd be surprised what soap, water, paint and elbow-grease can achieve," declared Will's mother, firing a sardonic look towards Carrie and her husband.

"Well, Carrie," asked Will as he squeezed her hand, "what do you think?"

What did she think? She thought it was just wonderful. It offered a way out of their dilemma. Yes, she could clean this place up. She could even learn how to redecorate the walls without getting paint all over the place. Yet all she could say to Will was, "But can we afford it?"

A wry smile crossed her fiancé's face before he conceded, "Probably not. But at least let's go and inquire."

Emma hid her disappointment well when Will and Carrie entered the office to return the keys of 105. She'd been so looking forward to meeting Sam again that she taken great pains over her grooming. There was just something, she felt, that was so magical about him. She had never been so taken with a young man before. He was so refreshing – no airs and graces: just raw, bewitching charm.

"I don't suppose there's anyone who could talk to us about the house, is there?" Will asked.

Switching on the intercom, Emma promptly announced, "Daddy, there's a couple here who are interested in the house at 105 Cornhill Terrace. Are you able to see them?"

Within seconds, Emma's father opened an adjoining door and beckoned them into the privacy of his inner sanctum where he indicated they should take a seat. In Carrie's eyes, he looked more like a benevolent confidant than a shrewd lawyer.

"So you are interested in putting in an offer for 105 Cornhill Terrace?"

"Not quite," said Will. "You see, we *would* like it but we can't really afford it."

Mr Stuart pulled some paper towards him, lifted his pen and sat ready to write. "How much would you be offering?"

Will hesitated. Carrie just gulped. Neither spoke.

"The asking price is thirteen hundred pounds," said the lawyer gently.

Carrie eyes widened. Sam had told them eleven hundred and fifty at the most! There was no way they could afford this house. She made to stand up.

Mr Stuart motioned to her to sit down again. "However, I do believe that you wish us to put a bid of eleven hundred to our clients. Is that correct?"

"Yes. But would we get a mortgage?" Will now looked at Carrie who nodded agreement. "And how much would the legal fees be?"

For the next five minutes, Will answered all Mr Stuart's questions. How much did he earn? For it was his earnings alone that the building society would consider, since what the wife earned wouldn't be counted. And how much would Will be allotting to Carrie?

Mr Stuart was astute. He altered figures here and there on Will's salary to allow for his free food on board ship and for standby payments; so that it finally appeared his annual pay amounted to three hundred and thirty five pounds. That meant they could be granted a mortgage of three times that amount – one thousand pounds. The deposit of one hundred and ten pounds they had already almost saved up and, by foregoing some extravagances, they could just about make it. But as for the legal fees – these were beyond the couple's means. Until, that was, Mr Stuart agreed to allow them to pay his fees up at so much per month over the next year.

Carrie felt the tears springing to her eyes. Here she was, a wee lassie born in the worst of Leith's slums, about to become the owner of a house in Cornhill Terrace no less. Then she remembered that no one had said what the monthly mortgage would be. "And h-how much would we have to p-pay the Building Society every month?" she stammered.

Mr Stuart smiled, "*Just* seven pounds, three shillings and eight pence."

Will winced. Carrie swallowed hard, thinking it might be *just* pennies to Mr Stuart but to her it was a fortune.

Rachel was surprised when Carrie withdrew a three-inch wide satin sash and two artificial yellow roses from a paper bag. "What on earth are you going to do with these?" her mother demanded.

"Sew the roses on to the sash and – see?" said Carrie, lifting up Hannah's white prayer book and holding the satin ribbon so that it hung down.

"I don't understand. You've ordered a bridal bouquet of roses for yourself and a posy for Alice. So why d'you need a prayer book as well . . . and a Catholic one at that?"

"Simple. I need something borrowed – that's the prayer book and, because I've had to cut back to get the deposit for the house, I went to Dick the florist on Great Junction Street and cancelled the flowers."

"But you really wanted to walk down the aisle carrying a bouquet of yellow roses."

Sniffing slightly, Carrie added, "Aye, and I was going to go out to Mount Vernon and put them on Granny's grave before I left on my honeymoon. But know something, Mum? I just know that getting the house will have pleased Granny Rosie more than a bunch of flowers."

"It certainly pleases me more," acknowledged Rachel, who began to wonder if Carrie was at last acquiring a well-overdue dose of common sense.

7

CUP FEVER AND COLD FEET

As Sam turned into C Division's Headquarters at Torphichen Place, it wasn't the Co-operative bus standing at the main entrance that he first noticed. No – it was Sandy, the Edinburgh City Police team manager who was standing, arms akimbo, out on the main road. Catching a glimpse of Sam he made such an exaggerated play of consulting his watch that Sam broke into an obligatory sprint.

"The coo's tail's decided to grace us with his presence at long last, eh? So we can mebbe get off now," Sandy called out as he made towards the bus.

"Look, I was supposed to finish my shift at five this morning but I didn't get away until six thirty," Sam explained defensively.

"And for why was that?"

"Well, didn't some daft numptie decide he could walk on water and tried it at Leith docks. What else could I do but jump in and save him?"

"Look, laddie! Our leaving for Cambridge on the stroke o eight was o much more importance – so you should just have left him to find out for himself if he was Almighty Jesus or no!"

Slightly shamefaced but without saying another word, Sam jumped on board to a chorus of derisive howls and whoops from his seated team-mates.

Following hard on his heels, Sandy allowed Sam to get settled in beside Billy Nicholson who proposed that since Sam had been working all night he'd be better able to get a bit of shut-eye if he took the inside seat. Once all the kerfuffle of seat changing had taken place, Sandy raised both hands for silence and prepared to address his team.

Billy leant over and whispered in Sam's ear, "You listen. This'll be the bit where Sandy digs up guid auld Robert the Bruce."

"Now, lads," began Sandy impressively, "this week we have the opportunity to cover ourselves in glory."

"Told you so!" said Billy, nudging Sam who was already beginning to nod off. "And I bet you he'll go on with 'Now's the day and now's the hour': ye ken – the bit where Sandy 'sees the front of battle lour'."

Sam only shook his head and sighed wearily.

"Oh aye," continued Sandy, quite oblivious to Billy's remarks. "Never in the history of the British Cup has a team from Scotland won it!"

"Just coming now to the wee bit where he requests that we drain our dearest veins and lay the proud usurpers low before finally . . ."

"The hopes and wishes of not only all the officers – including our Chief here in Edinburgh City – but the whole of Scotland's police forces are also behind us!" Sandy paused before uttering solemnly: "Remember, boys, these words from *Scots Wha Hae*, that urge us to 'do or die'!"

"When it comes to dying," sniggered Billy, "he means *he's* going to do himself in if the team don't deliver the goods!"

Sam made no reply but wrapped his arms tightly around himself and was fast asleep before the bus signalled it was pulling out and heading for Cambridge. He remained blissfully unaware of Sandy's final warning – that no alcohol was to be consumed by any team member until after the victory!

Excitement on the day of the match had reached fever pitch. Sandy was right about the whole of the Edinburgh force being behind the team. Not only had Sir William Morren, the Chief Constable, flown down to attend the game but so also had his very able deputy, Mr Roy.

The teams took their places on Cambridge City Football Stadium's perfect pitch. Sam generally used any game of football to relieve his pent-up tensions but today he felt under special pressure to succeed. He knew that Sandy had seen to it that the Edinburgh squad was fully prepared and had personally made sure that every player was fit, disciplined, and trained to such a peak that they could have completed a marathon and still had the breath to run on.

Once the whistle blew, Sam's daydreaming stopped abruptly and battle commenced. Within minutes of the first tentative exchanges, Sam realised that the Cambridge City Police Team would prove to be no walk-over. They too were a top-class team, with five ex-professionals in their ranks, and they were hungry, *very* hungry, for victory. Added to this, they had a support group of at least five and a half thousand to cheer them on from the terracing, whereas Edinburgh City Police had only the Chief with his deputy and six other stalwarts, who had been fully prepared to spend three days of their leave to fill up the few remaining seats on the bus and urge them on to victory.

Nonetheless, ten minutes into the match, Sam realised that even though Cambridge had the more experienced side they did not play as a fully co-ordinated team, which meant that their front line seldom moved in cohesion and no one among their forwards seemed to know exactly what to do with the ball. The Edinburgh men on the other hand *did* look as if they knew where they were going but the goals they needed constantly eluded them. The result was that by the interval there had been no scoring in what was a somewhat lacklustre game. Both sides had failed to take advantage of several good chances. The second half began no better and Edinburgh became despondent when Alistair, their centre-forward and most prolific goal-scorer, injured an ankle and was left limping for the rest of the match. Fifteen minutes later, Peter at inside-left hurt his knee; and this succession of mishaps gave rise to a feeling of hopelessness and a growing realisation that all they could do was to struggle on with nine fit men. They could merely play a wholly defensive game, with the aim of limiting the extent of what seemed an inevitable defeat. Miracles do sometimes happen, however, and hopes rose when Jimmy, at outside-right, scored the first goal of the match after a brilliant right-wing manoeuvre down the by-line. The Edinburgh team were now one up in the sixty-fifth minute! Two minutes later, expectations went sky-high when the ball landed at the feet of the injured Alistair, who promptly dummied the opposing centre-half by letting the ball run between his legs. Cleverly anticipating the move, Sam ran on to the ball and prodded it neatly past the goalkeeper as the pair collided. Lying spread-eagled on the ground, both men turned their heads to watch the ball trickle with agonising slowness across the goal line. The handicapped Edinburgh team now had simply to defend their two-goal cushion and this they did admirably until the final eight minutes when Tommy, the centre-half, who was determined to foil a fierce late rally by Cambridge, grew so excited that he headed the ball into his own goal, thus giving Cambridge the belief that they might still win. Johnny at right-half, unable to believe what had happened, fell down and lay seemingly comatose. When the trainer ran on to the field to ask what was wrong he wearily replied, "I just couldn't believe it so I thought I'd hae a wee rest."

Despite the constant pressure of the final minutes, Edinburgh held on valiantly to achieve a great victory. The moment the final whistle went, Sandy led the small Scottish supporting contingent on to the field to join in the wild jubilation of the team players – oblivious to the fact that a week's wages of loose change was cascading merrily from his un-flapped jacket pockets. The jumping, whooping and back-slapping only drew to a close once the Edinburgh captain, Jock Fyfe, had been summoned amidst thunderous applause to receive the cup.

The Edinburgh squad and supporters who sluggishly boarded the bus the following morning looked as if they had lost the match. Sleep deprivation, over-indulgence in alcohol and the desire to be contortionists on the dance floor had all taken their toll. Sam had even broken his pledge of abstinence, as he simply couldn't refuse to drink some champagne from the trophy cup. He even went on to have a pint of shandy, which, to his amazement, he found very refreshing!

Once aboard the bus he again settled down in an inside seat. Within minutes Billy dropped down beside him and Sam was surprised to hear him remark, "That's twice in a month I've seen ye excel yourself."

"What d'ye mean?"

"Well," explained Billy, "ye just did dandy yesterday and a month ago was it no you that was a real swank giving your sister away?"

Sam nudged him playfully. "Aye that was some wedding, right enough." His thoughts turned back to all that had happened on that memorable day when Carrie was married. He knew there were so many things about it that he would never forget. One was how innocent and angelic Carrie had looked in her hand-made dress. And, as she'd taken his arm and proceeded down the central aisle of Pilrig-Dalmeny Church, he felt that her prayer book with its satin ribbon adorned with two artificial yellow roses added a special touch to the picture. He honestly believed that a large bouquet would somehow have looked out of place. He'd remember also how Alice, beautiful Alice, had looked in her flowing lilac dress and how she'd tossed her head disdainfully, as if declaring that the lack of a posy to carry had cheapened the whole effect. Sam smiled to himself as he recalled her making a dolly bag out of the scraps of material left over from her dress and how handy it had come in for holding Carrie's spectacles – specs that were needed not only for Carrie to sign the register but also to see where to put her name! But, as he watched the countryside of Cambridge flying past, Sam acknowledged it wasn't his sisters who had been the main focus of his attention in the church. It had been his mother, Rachel, who in Sam's opinion had stolen the show when she'd walked down the aisle dressed in a light-brown suit, complemented by an elegant fox fur. Sam thought she looked more imposing even than Princess Marina. He'd always marvelled at the grace and dress-sense of his mother: she had that *je ne sais quoi* that made him so proud of her.

Thankfully the whole wedding service had gone without a single hitch. It was when they were outside that the first problem arose. There appeared to be two photographers present, both clicking away like mad. This wouldn't have mattered if the unofficial one hadn't pitched up at the reception and begun taking orders from the assembled guests at six shillings a time, a shilling less than the official photographer would be charging. Fortunately, Sam's Auntie Bella accosted the impostor and demanded, "You asking me to pay you for a photo I haven't seen?"

"No problem, madam," the man had suavely responded. "You'll have the choice of ten and if you don't like any of them you'll get a full refund."

Thereupon the oily character found himself being roughly dragged backwards by his jacket collar and, skewing his head round to protest, found himself face to face with Sam.

"Well, well, if it's no Tricky Dickie. Now, just empty out your pockets and gie all the money back. And," added Sam, with a snort, "I've already sent for the Gayfield polis."

As the money was grudgingly being tossed on the table, Sam loosened his grip on the man's collar so that he could check the amount. Seizing his chance, Tricky Dickie jumped nimbly to his feet and scampered out of the hall.

"Ye ken him?" Auntie Bella asked.

"Oh aye," said Sam with a grin. "He tries that swiz all the time. Nae spool in the camera and gullible folk faw for it every time. Then he just runs away with their dosh."

The reception, however, was a great success, with every-body enjoying their steak pie and trifle; and when the ceilidh band started up, the whole company was ready for a knees-up. It was while Sam was partnering his mother in an Eightsome Reel that he glanced over to the door and was surprised to see Emma Stuart standing there. He'd met her down in Charlotte Street two days before and had suggested she come along to the reception. As soon as the reel was finished, Sam dashed to the door to greet Emma and introduce her to all the family. Paul simply drooled in ecstasy when he was introduced to her and, with a Strip the Willow just start-ing up, he grabbed her hand and hauled her on to the dance floor. Sam could only stare in amazement when Emma, like all the other lady dancers, took off her shoes so that she too could safely birl her way through the tumultuous dance.

All too soon the time came for Will and Carrie to leave. Now smartly dressed in a new grey twill coat with matching hat, Carrie stood halfway down the stairs waving to everyone and wholly unable to hide her joy and excitement.

Their taxi drew up in Queen Street just outside the Kintore Rooms and the driver impatiently sounded his horn. With a final wave to her mother and siblings, Carrie sedately stepped in, followed by Will.

"Where to?" asked the taxi driver.

"Oh, blow it!" exclaimed Will. "I completely forgot to book somewhere. Can you suggest a hotel?"

"Money no object?"

"We-ell," Will said uncertainly, "I couldn't quite stretch to the Caley, the Waverley or the George – but I want something better than a doss-house."

"And as far as I'm concerned," croaked a tearful Carrie, "it has to have a cold, a *really* cold floor."

The taxi driver opened his mouth to ask why but, thinking better of it, switched on the engine and headed for the Old Town. After a ten-minute drive, he deposited Will and Carrie at the entrance to the Cockburn Hotel. "Think you'll find the floor and everywhere else in this hotel is well below zero."

Some time later, Will proved to be at a complete loss to understand why, after they had made love, Carrie jumped out of bed and stood for five whole minutes on the cold floor while drinking a glass of cold water. One outcome of this bizarre behaviour, however, was that when Carrie got back into bed she was shivering so much that Will obviously had to warm his bride up – an action which naturally resulted in Carrie having to jump out of bed once more to stand on the chilly floor. Being by now enthusiastically encouraged by Will, the whole performance was repeated four times!

The following morning, Will and Carrie skipped breakfast but did manage to catch the train for Perth where they were going to spend their three-day honeymoon at the Station Hotel. Being waited on hand and foot by Will and the hotel staff suited Carrie admirably and helped bring true her dream of what a honeymoon should be like. Indeed, she was so deeply in love that she readily agreed to Will's proposal that they should go to Dundee for the afternoon to catch the football match. He rewarded her by taking her to tea in Keiller's tearoom where she gorged herself on toasted muffins and marmalade.

Before they knew it, the dream was over. Wednesday morning arrived and they were on their way back to Edinburgh. As soon as they reached Will's home, his mother produced a telegram for him. "Came this morning," she said smugly.

Will grimaced as he tore open the envelope and his face fell. "Says I'm to join a ship in Manchester by Thursday."

"But that means you'll have to leave tonight," wailed Carrie.

"So he will," his mum chipped in, "thanks to having you to keep *and* a mortgage, not to mention having a house to furnish."

Carrie wanted to say that she could keep herself, as she always had done, but stayed silent, realising that there was a plus in everything. At least she wouldn't have to spend a nuptial night under Mrs Fraser's roof!

It was past ten o'clock when Carrie arrived at her own mother's house. She did try to open the door with her key but as the snib was down she had to knock. The door was opened by Rachel who was amazed to see her daughter standing there on her own.

"No Will?" her mother asked, craning her neck to peer further into the stairwell. Carrie shook her head and tears began to cascade down her cheeks.

"You've not left him already?"

"No," sobbed Carrie. "*He* left me!"

"He *what*?" exclaimed Rachel.

"Oh, Mum, he had to catch the nine o'clock train for Manchester."

Rachel relaxed when it dawned on her that Will had left to join a ship. "Never you mind. I've got some good news for you." Carrie stopped sniffing and looked enquiringly at her mother.

"Aye. Know how you gave up your wee job in the picture house?"

"Uh-huh."

"Well, Sam happened to be passing there today when the manager came out and asked him to tell you that you could go back even if you wanted to do just two week-nights and Saturday."

Carrie shook her head sadly. She had hoped that once she became Mrs Fraser she wouldn't need to hold down two jobs but, with so much needed for the house in Cornhill Terrace, she would simply have to go back to that. After all, she hadn't really got what she wanted in the way of wedding presents: no Acme wringer, no iron; not even an ironing board. Just eight yellow dusters, ten pairs of towels and sixteen pairs of white sheets that she confided to Auntie Bella wasn't what she actually wanted. Auntie Bella, being the woman she was, had replied tartly that Carrie should be very grateful – especially because, provided she left them in their wrappings, she could always pawn them when she was hard up.

Mrs Mack was the chief usherette and in charge of the main medium-priced seating at the Palace Picture House. She and Carrie had become good friends over the several years they'd worked together – so much so that whenever Carrie came on duty Mrs Mack would install Carrie in their cubby-hole where she always had a flask of hot tea and some fish paste sandwiches ready for her.

On the Monday night when Carrie arrived to resume her duties, Mrs Mack was obviously in a high state of excitement. Could it be, wondered Carrie, that it was all down to her return? But it turned out to be more than that. While pouring out the tea, Mrs Mack announced that this was a special week with all the films having Jennifer Jones in the starring role.

"You mean we're having her latest – *Love Is a Many-Splendoured Thing*?" squealed Carrie, unable to keep her enthusiasm in check.

Mrs Mack nodded. "Aye, from Thursday. But for three days, starting the night, we're re-showing *The Song of Bernadette*!"

Carrie wanted to groan but instead she took a deep breath. Two years ago they'd featured, at Mrs Mack's insistence, a re-run of that film. And the problem was that Mrs Mack was a devout Catholic. First of all, she had refused to allow the courting couples to sit in the chummy seats as there was to be no impropriety whilst such a holy film was being shown. Then she had opened the back door and sneaked in any of the priests or nuns from the local church – St Mary's Star of the Sea – who wanted to see the film. And when the final scenes appeared, featuring the agonising and prolonged death of Bernadette, she'd knelt down in the main aisle at every showing and joined the stars on screen in their prayers and rosaries! Carrie would then have to assist Mrs Mack to her feet when she'd been knocked down by the stampede of people rushing to catch their bus home. "Oh, Carrie!" she'd wail. "See all the suffering and agonies that lassie endured? No wonder they made her a saint!" After the first showing Carrie felt she too knew what suffering was all about!

Carrie wondered whether she should suggest that Mrs Mack might kneel down at the foot of the aisle and so avoid being knocked over. But would she listen? Being carried away by religious films was not Mrs Mack's only eccentricity. She was positively obsessed with keeping out the two well-known child molesters who frequented the picture houses in Leith. Those two small, seedy-looking men were banned from all the local cinemas but somehow always seemed to find their way in. In the Palace's case, it was because one-eyed Andra Scullen, who was in charge of the cheapest seats, never seemed to recognise them. While Carrie was on her honeymoon, Mrs Mack had spied one of the pair slinking into her part of the auditorium, and had followed her usual routine. First she banged him smartly on the shoulder with her rubber torch and then, hauling him out of his seat by the scruff of his neck, bundled him towards the back door and kicked him unceremoniously out into Duke Street. Unfortunately, when landing on the pavement he had collided with a hawker pushing his barrow. The police were called to deal with the resulting fracas and the child molester duly made a counter-complaint against Mrs Mack for assault. Sam had been asked to deal with the matter and, on questioning Mrs Mack, she had replied, "Look here, Sam Campbell. Every time I ask you to deal with they two weirdoes you tell me you need corroborating evidence. The bairns can't give us that, 'cause they're too scared to testify. So what corroborating evidence have you against me? My torch cannae talk?"

Carrie had no need to worry about the film that night. Only twenty people turned up to see it so Carrie was able to stretch out on the chummy seats and doze off. She was just so tired these days! Cleaning up the Cornhill Terrace house, for which she now had the keys, was just so utterly exhausting.

The cubby-hole that Mrs Mack and Carrie used for their breaks was just a large walk-in cupboard with a wooden recess housing a bench that two people could just squeeze on to. Mrs Mack had made the recess comfortable by providing cushions, a crocheted knee blanket and a small occasional table that sat in front of the bench.

On Easter Saturday, Carrie had been first to take her break but when she didn't return to the auditorium within twenty minutes Mrs Mack went looking for her. The first place she investigated was naturally the cubby-hole and, on opening the door, she was surprised to find Carrie fast asleep, her head slumped upon the bench and the blanket tucked in over her knees. However, it was only when she saw that Carrie hadn't drunk any of her tea nor eaten her sandwiches that she became really concerned. Walking over, she gently tapped the sleeping Carrie. "C'mon, lassie," she coaxed. "Whit's wrang wi ye?"

Carrie reluctantly willed herself awake and yawned, "Where am I?"

"Ye're in the Palace and you should be out there on the floor – you ken how thae bairns get oot o control when Tarzan's on. Listen to that! Them that are over eight are jumping on the seats beating their chests and howlin', 'Me Tarzan. You Jane.' And them that are under seven think they're chimpanzees and are swinging on onything they can find, screamin', 'Me Cheetah!' – and firing banana skins all ower the place."

Rising and stretching heself, Carrie muttered, "Okay."

"Aye, but it's no okay, is it? Just look at you."

Carrie peered at herself in the mirror that was nailed to the back of the door. A white sickly face with sunken eyes was all she could see. "I've had this sickness thing for weeks now. Nearly fainted this morning, so I did."

"Aye, but you expect that when you're . . ." Mrs Mack stopped and pointed meaningfully at Carrie's stomach.

Carrie began to laugh. "I'm not expecting, Mrs Mack. Will's been away for six weeks now."

"So? You had a honeymoon, didn't ye?"

"Aye. But I took precautions."

"Like what?"

Carrie went on to explain how Bernie had told her about jumping out of bed and standing on the cold floor. Now it was Mrs Mack's turn to start cackling. "Don't tell me your mammy never told you that there's only one way no to fall wi a bairn and that's . . . no to do it!"

Shaking her head, Carrie explained, "My Mum never talks about these things."

"You mean she's no even noticed that you're puking up all the time."

"I don't puke all the time."

"Naw? Then what happened when you went out over the road to Elio's for the chips last night?"

Bowing her head in an attempt to hide the intense flush of embarrassment that was overtaking her, Carrie replied, "I told you there must have been something wrong with the fat they were using. The smell was disgusting. No wonder I vomited!"

Before Mrs Mack could speak, a loud knock sounded at the door. "Look, you two. If ye're any longer in there, we'll need to send for a posse to round up the bairns who are now chasing each other all over the place with the DDT spray."

Carrie was about to dash out of the door but Mrs Mack held her back. "It's his DDT spray, so let him get killed trying to get it back. See here," Mrs Mack delved into her knitting bag and withdrew some two-ply white wool and a pattern, "I'll show you how to knit a shawl."

Carrie shook her head vehemently. "I'm *not* expecting!"

"Okay, Carrie. But just promise me that you'll take a sample o your pee down to the doctor and if he says you're no . . . then I'll eat this wool!"

"You're on. But what'll I take it in?"

Mrs Mack rolled her eyes. "A jam jar, of course. But a wee one. No a two-pound one!"

Sam was wandering round his beat in a dilly-dally daydream. He truly couldn't believe that ever since Carrie's wedding he and Emma Stuart had been walking out together. She was so unlike any other girl he'd ever known. He had expected her to be all hoity-toity – full of airs and graces – but she was such good fun and always game for a laugh. She hadn't even turned down an invitation to meet him, when he'd finished his nightshift, this morning at six o'clock. The plan was that they would then climb romantic Arthur's Seat, albeit by the easy route, to take part in the May Day service and then to wash their faces in the morning dew. This was a ritual that had been going on for centuries. Lassies actually believed that by washing their faces in the dew they would become beautiful. Carrie, who was desperate on her wedding day to look better than Ingrid Bergman, had tried it last year but all she'd ended up with was a fat lip when she tripped over a boulder.

Before starting their descent, Sam and Emma stood hand-in-hand gazing at the panoramic view of the historic city. They marvelled at the rosy hue that hung over the skyline as the sun began to rise. Hands still locked together, they made their way down the rough path. Sam took a deep breath and wondered if this was the right time to ask Emma the question that had been keeping him awake at nights. A rabbit dashing for its burrow startled Emma and she squeezed hard on Sam's hand. That was the opportunity for him to speak. As he steadied her, he said, "Emma, I've been thinking. You and me get on so well thegither . . . how about us getting married?"

Letting go of Sam's hand Emma drew back. "Married! But Sam, you just don't suddenly get married, you have to plan – make arrangements." She hesitated before adding, "For a start we would need a house. Where would we get one?"

"Easy. They're building a new housing scheme at Clermiston and they're putting in lots o Police Houses. I could put my name down for one."

"A housing scheme?" queried Emma. "But whatever would my mother say?"

"You mean your dad?"

"No. My mother. But let me think about it first." She then tucked her arm through Sam's and asked, "Am I more beautiful now than before I washed in the dew?"

"No way, Emma, could the dew improve you!"

It was never unusual for Sam to pop into Carrie's for a cup of tea when he was doing his rounds – but not at midnight. Sitting in an easy chair and staring into space, Carrie wasn't even startled when Sam abruptly walked in. "Used my key," he said, as he sank into the chair opposite. "Saw your light was on so wondered if something was up?"

Carrie puffed. "You could say that."

"So?"

"Know who's expecting?"

"Aye, Hannah. Mammy's been going on and on about it ever since the letter arrived."

The news about Hannah jolted Carrie. "Hannah's expecting *again*? But Morag'll just be going on three."

"It's Hannah's life. So why are you getting yourself in such a stooshie about it?"

"It's no Hannah expecting that's the big problem . . . it's what *I'm* going to do!"

"You?"

"Aye, due in December, that stupid doctor says. I never should have listened to Mrs Mack. Should have stayed happy in my ignorance."

Carrie now lifted a large sheet of paper from her knees. "This here is the list of all the things I still need for this house. Now I'll have to add on a pram, a cot, a baby bath, nappies and smocks."

"To the bottom of the list?"

"No!" Carrie brandished the paper angrily. "As this here is a five-year plan, these things'll have to go to the top . . . and when I stop working and the plan extends to ten years, I'll need to add a school bag, a duffle-coat and some wellies – somewhere in the middle!"

Sam rose and went into the galley kitchen, which was just off the living room, and filled the kettle. "Fancy a cup?"

"Well, as I can't sleep for worry, I might as well. Oh Sam, how on earth am I going make ends meet?"

Sam turned to frame the doorway. "You're no doing so badly."

"Badly!" she scoffed. "Look, I'd have nothing if you and Mum hadn't bought the bed, and if Will's mum hadn't suddenly pitched in with the wherewithal so I could get a dining table, chairs and sideboard."

Trying to lift Carrie's spirits, Sam said, "Well, these two easy chairs of yours are hardly nothing."

"But I'm paying them up over two years. Anyway, forget my problems. What are you doing here at this time of night, Sam?"

"As I said, I saw your light and I needed someone to talk to."

"About?"

"Emma. I made a mistake, Carrie."

"Oh, God! She's no expecting too?"

"Naw. If she was – well, I'd be as happy as a sand-boy." Carrie knew this was not the time to say anything. "I asked her to marry me. Told her I could get a police house in Clermiston. That was last week and she's not been in touch ever since."

"So you don't know if it's yes or no?"

Sam shook his head. "It's neither. It's maybe. You see, I met her father in the street and he says that, when you've been brought up in Murrayfield and educated at Mary Erskine's Ladies, a police house in Clermiston is no quite where she'd be happy."

"But what does Emma say?"

Sam shrugged his shoulders. "I don't know. And I can't ask her because she's now been shipped away up north to her mammy's folk."

"Oh, I see. So that's that!"

With a sniff, Sam interrupted his sister. "All isn't lost though. Ye see, her dad – and he's a really nice honest man, Carrie – did say to wait two years and, if we still feel the same about each other and if I've something better tae offer than a police house in Clermiston, he'll no stand in our way."

Carrie nodded. "Two years is . . ."

"I ken what ye're thinking, Carrie. But I'd wait twenty years for Emma. And in the meantime I'm going to be saving up a deposit for a guid house in a guid district. Remember how Mammy used to take us walking round bungalow land in Craigentinny every Sunday; and every Sunday she'd say in that dreamy voice of hers, 'Know something? One day one of you kids might be rich enough to live here'." Sam breathed in deeply and as his chest expanded his hopes rose and he declared: "That's it, a bungalow in Craigentinny is what I'll get for my Emma!"

8

MIXED BLESSINGS

"Well?" demanded Sam of his sister. "What d'you think?"

Desperate to find some words of encouragement, Carrie carefully surveyed the bungalow that nestled just beyond the boundary of Craigentinny Golf Course and whose front door directly faced the Council refuse dump. What could she say about a garden that was now a wilderness and a house in a state of complete disrepair? Its filthy window frames looked weary and unloved – and yet these were maybe the easiest problem to deal with. "Suppose some paint and elbow grease would make a difference."

"Aye," Sam enthused. "I just knew it. Like me, ye can see the potential. And as I've been saving for . . ." Sam paused.

"Five years, isn't it?" Carrie reminded.

Both felt that five years was a long time to save up for a dream. For the first two years Sam had been driven by his desire to get a bungalow for his beloved Emma. That was motivation enough until he opened the *Edinburgh Evening News* one Saturday night and found himself staring in disbelief at Emma's wedding photograph. She'd married a professional gent in the banking world who just happened to have a knighthood and who could provide her with a luxury mansion at Blackhall, in keeping with her social ambitions. Sam smiled ruefully at the memory. At the outset he'd given the marriage one year – and only one – because he was quite positive that once Emma found out what *he* knew about Sir James Souter she'd surely be thinking it would have been far better to have settled for Sam and a police house in Clermiston. But Sam didn't realise that Emma would never come back to him because outward appearances were more important to her than true happiness.

Carrie broke into his thoughts. "I know fine you could make a palace out of this house in time, Sam, but if Emma ever did come back to you would she really want to be confronted every day by the reek from that rubbish dump – not to mention the pong from the Seafield sewage works!"

Sam laughed. "She'd feel right at home, she would. After all, didn't she marry a heap o garbage in the first place. Anyway," he added, looking towards the tip, "the football pitches are in front o it."

Carrie smiled at her brother. There lay all the football pitches, right enough. And she knew that when the local laddies were out playing Sam would be there also, coaching and spurring them on. "I suppose you're getting it for a song?"

"Aye, two thousand, seven hundred; and I've got fifteen hundred o that already saved up."

Without answering, Carrie looked about the garden and suddenly realised that her four-year-old daughter had disappeared. "Sophie! Sophie!" she yelled, but only a solitary blackbird chirping in the rowan tree responded to her cry. "Where on earth could she have gone, Sam?"

They both dashed towards the side of the house but stopped in their tracks when they saw that the front door now lay wide open and Sophie was in the hall playing with a German Shepherd puppy.

"Came with the house, did it?" Carrie asked.

"Naw, naw! But as Mammy doesn't want to come and bide with me, I thought a dog would be company – besides guarding the house."

With a nod, Carrie silently acknowledged that Emma's rejection still hurt Sam deeply. At least that bonnie bitch standing there in the doorway would always be loyal to him.

"Uncle Sam, could I have the *other* puppy," Sophie wheedled, pulling vigorously at Sam's trouser leg.

"What other puppy?" screeched Carrie.

Sam shifted uneasily, "Och, she's just on about a wee runt frae a collie litter that I took aff the breeder's hand."

Sophie immediately dashed into the kitchen and emerged a few moments later carrying the small black and white pup. "Oh please, Mummy, could we get one? *Please*!"

"A dog in our home?" queried Carrie, thinking to herself that it *had* been a home last week but now that dry rot had been discovered it was like a demolition site. And it wasn't the mess that worried her. That could be cleared up; but where, oh where, was she going to find the five hundred pounds to pay the contractors? No wonder she was always feeling sick and tired these days. Until then, life had seemed to be fine. They were just managing, thanks to Carrie doing night shifts on Fridays and Saturdays as an auxiliary nurse at the Eastern General. It wasn't a job she particularly liked – wiping backsides and emptying bedpans was hardly an upward career move – but the reason she did it was that there was always somebody at Learig Close on a Saturday, eager to look after Sophie so that she herself could have a decent sleep.

Her thoughts went back to three weeks ago when Will had phoned from Garston to say that his ship would be docked there for five days and could she and Sophie come down. How much she'd enjoyed her time there! All the meals cooked for her and they'd gone to the pictures. Okay, so it was just *The Wizard of Oz* and they'd both seen that many times before, but Sophie hadn't; and the wonderful time they'd spent together had them believing they really were all on the Yellow Brick Road. These warm memories had Carrie feeling deeply grateful that her marriage hadn't become a humdrum affair, as seemed to be the case with so many of her friends – but after all, she and Will hadn't spent much time together since he was so often away at sea. And once she got around to telling him about the dry rot, she knew he'd say that would mean him staying on at sea for another couple of years till they were really back on their feet.

On their feet? Carrie stared cynically down at her own feet. All her life she'd never really been off those two feet, yet somehow she'd never really been securely on them.

"Ken what? There's still another wee runt looking for a hame in the collie litter, Carrie," mumbled Sam, whose heartstrings were being pulled by his niece's pleas. "I could ask the breeder if he'd gie it to ye at a knock-down price."

"Sam, please don't start. You know the hole I'm in with the blasted dry rot. Don't you realise that I'm probably going to have to do another night at the hospital? So there's simply no way I can look after a pup – never mind feed it."

"But, Mummy," interposed Sophie, "when I told Mrs Berry . . ."

"Who's Mrs Berry?" asked Sam.

"Sophie's teacher at Links Place Nursery School," explained Carrie.

"She said," continued Sophie, "that even though you've got dry rot, Mummy, it wasn't serious and your legs wouldn't fall off."

Carrie rolled her eyes upwards as she thought how much simpler it would have been if it was she who had the rot and not the house. And maybe, just maybe, she wouldn't be feeling as sick as she was.

Rachel sat staring blankly into space, thinking that here again her children were doing what suited *them* best, with no consideration for what might suit their mother. Wringing her hands till they hurt, she accepted that her auld enemy – that black, satanic spectre of depression – was about to swallow her up once more. She knew she just couldn't face another spell as a voluntary patient in the Andrew Duncan Clinic. She'd no choice but to battle on by herself to keep the enemy in check. How to do it? Well, first she'd buy a bottle of Neurophosphate which in the past had stopped her getting too bad. She grimaced as she recalled the bright green liquid that tasted so awful: but it was a taste she'd willingly put up with if it helped her to hold on. She admitted she was luckier now than when her bairns had been wee – at least she could afford to buy the stuff nowadays. Used to be just half a crown, she mused – a pittance now but pretty well out of her reach back then. So desperate she'd been in those days that she'd willingly pawn anything simply to buy the bottle that saved her from being subjected to yet another barbaric session of electrotherapy. She shuddered at the memory. Twice a week for six weeks had seen her firmly strapped down upon the hospital bed. No anaesthetic to dull the excruciating pain, no muscle-relaxant to help her cope with the convulsive jerking of her whole body – seizures that left her quite unable to control her bodily functions. And the loss of memory that took such a time to recover. She smiled grimly, remembering how the consultant psychiatrist had said they didn't really know why ECT worked for the most difficult of depressive conditions. They just knew that somehow it did. Eight weeks of last year she'd been in that blasted hospital. Moreover, it had cost her the decent job she'd had at the Queen's. And now she was earning a living by looking after an old woman in nearby Restalrig Avenue while her sons were at work; and then, in the evening, by being in charge of the cocoa and Horlicks trolley at the Eastern General.

By now, Rachel had become so engrossed in those unpleasant memories that she didn't hear the outside door opening and a voice calling out, "Coo-ee, it's only me."

Bella seated herself unceremoniously and felt the teapot to see if it was still warm. Reassured, she shook it to see if there was enough left for a cuppa. It was only when she pushed back the chair to go and light the gas under the kettle that Rachel realised someone was there – Bella, to whom she owed so much and whom she could always depend upon to come and be with her, yet who in most ways was quite ineffectual. If only Bella had been more like Rachel's beloved Auntie Anna, who had brought her up from infancy after her own mother had died in the Leith Poorhouse that was now the Eastern General Hospital. Auntie Anna had been the wise old woman who attended to all the hatching and dispatching within the condemned slum tenement at 18 Couper Street where they'd all lived – Auntie Anna, with her own three lassies and Rachel, all in one room and kitchen, where the only luxuries were a cold water tap and a commode (strictly for night use only). And yet Anna had been willing to share that subsistence-level existence with Rachel, her friend's bairn, rather than see her put into the Poorhouse Orphanage.

"Feeling blue, are ye?" Bella asked, hoping that the glazed look in Rachel's eyes wasn't a sign she was getting bad again.

"Just thinking about Alice."

Bella smiled. "Aye, she'll be home in three months."

Rachel shook her head. "No, she won't."

"But she only went out to Canada for a year and my Cathie says she's awfy homesick, so she thought she wouldn't even last out the year."

"Aye, well, a letter this week tells me she's met a mounted policeman and she's in love."

"Right enough. I could fall for a Mountie. Real guid-looking they horses are."

"Well, it seems it was the man she fell for and not the horse," commented Rachel tartly.

"Just think yourself lucky! All three o my lassies went to Canada for a year or two and no ane o them came back. You've still got your other four bairns. And, ken something?" Bella turned, looked over her shoulder and smiled. Rachel knew this was the sign that Bella was about to communicate with her departed spirits.

"That was both our mammies that came through the now and they both say they can see us travelling thegither – off to Canada we are to visit them aw."

"They didn't say anything about sending us the fortune we'll need to get there, did they?"

"The spirit world's no concerned wi money. But . . ." Bella had to think fast. "Aye, they did say travelling would soon be a lot cheaper. Anyway you should be glad Alice is going to stay in Toronto – and with Paul a lawyer now ye'll soon be rolling in it."

"That's where you're wrong, Bella. Paul's qualified in law now right enough but he's not going to practise it. He's going into the police!"

"Could he no have jyned up at eighteen and saved ye putting yourself in the grubber to get him through uni-bloody-versity?"

"Well, not really. He'd have had to do his national service then."

Bella shrugged. "Pretty expensive way to bide out o a war if ye ask me. But your Paul always had such a high and mighty opinion o himself." It was then that Bella remembered she'd picked up a letter from the floor when she came in and she now laid it in front of Rachel. "Picked that aff yer floor." Bella lifted the letter up again and closely scrutinised the envelope. "Nice writing. Wish I could write like that."

Without a word, Rachel seized it from Bella's hand. She was right in guessing it was from Hannah. She knew she must open the envelope that, as Bella had noted, was addressed in the most beautiful script. Hannah's writing, of course. Her own Hannah, who'd always shown such promise at school. Rachel shook her head wearily as she slipped a knife under the flap of the envelope and slit it open. With a weary sigh she took out the single sheet of notepaper, already knowing what would be written there. It was sure to be what Hannah hadn't had the courage to tell her by telephone. Oh, that telephone! Such a great way it had been of keeping in touch with events in the Outer Hebrides. Every week Rachel would go down to Carrie's and wait, sometimes for hours, until Hannah found time to run to the callbox by the harbour and make her call. Last Sunday, Hannah had chatted gaily for ages to Rachel about everything – except that bairn number seven was on its way.

Rachel was still clutching the unread letter in her hand when Carrie walked in and joined the two women. "Mum!" she called out.

"Oh, it's you again," Rachel managed to croak. She looked straight at Carrie and saw that her face was drawn. Something was obviously worrying her. "Now, before you start, please don't go on about you having that dry rot."

"Mum, it's not me that has dry rot – it's the house. What *I* have is ..." Carrie hesitated before blurting it out "... financial embarrassment ... and ..."

"Dry rot?" said Bella with some relish. "Now that's a real bad thing. Everything faws off. But that's what ye get for haeing a bought house. Now if ye'd been content with a Corporation house – *they* never get dry rot, for they ken the Council hasnae the wherewithal to fix it."

Carrie and Rachel looked at each other and were both about to argue the point with Bella but wisely decided it was best to ignore her. Instead, Rachel firmly warned her daughter, "Look, Carrie, I've had quite enough this day from Paul, Alice and Hannah; so please don't *you* start."

"Aye," joined in Bella. "No tae mention that sooner o a pup o Sam's."

"Are you saying he's gone and got another dog, Auntie Bella?"

"No Carrie. It's the collie that's the sooner. Sooner pee on yer mother's new carpet than anywhere else."

Carrie allowed herself a slight giggle before Rachel went on. "Here's Alice going to marry a Canadian, Paul's joining the police, and Hannah's expecting again ..."

"And so am I, Mum," said Carrie, bursting into tears.

"What!" exclaimed Bella. "But your Will's been away six months. Oh, Carrie, when ye said ye were going to do a night-shift to pay for the dry rot I *didn't* think ye meant – oh, no, ye *couldn't*."

"Auntie Bella, just what *are* you suggesting? Mum, did you hear what she said? Are you going to let her away with it?" exclaimed Carrie, who had to continue unaided, since Rachel was ignoring her plea. "If you must know, Auntie Bella, my Will docked at Garston for five days and I went down to see him."

"Garston? Where the devil is Garston?" asked Bella, looking distinctly bewildered.

"South of Liverpool. And Liverpool, in case you don't know it, Auntie, is a big port in England."

"Oh, but Carrie, your neighbours will no know you've been to . . . wherever it is. So you'll ken fine what they'll be thinking!"

"No. What will they be thinking?"

"That you've had an affair. Or at best that you're like Hannah an over fond o you ken what."

"Don't be ridiculous, Auntie Bella. Sophie will be five when this baby is born. Mum, *please* tell her."

"But she's right, Carrie. You behaving like a wanton woman has got you expecting and how does that help you get your hands on the five hundred you need for the dry rot?"

Carrie snorted before haughtily replying, "The Building Society will lend us the money. But instead of being mortgage-free in twenty years, we'll be back to twenty-five years."

"So by the time you're fifty you'll maybe be debt-free."

Tears welled up in Carrie's eyes and she began to sob. "Yes, Mum. And now Will says it might be better if he stays on at sea until we're out of the grubber."

"Well, instead of greeting the way you're doing you should just count yourself lucky that you won't have a useless man around your feet."

"Mum, my Will's not useless!"

No one noticed that the outside door had opened again until an over-excited collie pup scampered into the kitchen. "Good grief!" exclaimed Rachel as the pup circled, jumped and urinated.

"Oh, the wee sooner," Bella chortled merrily as she bent down to pat the puppy.

Carrie huffed and puffed while Sam bounded into the kitchen with a washing cloth already in his hands. "Sorry, Mammy. I'll soon have her trained," wheedled Sam.

"No fast enough," retorted Rachel, remembering vividly how Sam, as a wee laddie, would always say, "Sorry, Mammy," whenever he'd displeased her.

"How's the polis job going, son?"

"Well, as ye know, Aunty Bella, I've passed all my promotion exams – sergeant and inspector – but I'm still waiting to be actually promoted."

"But your Mammy says ye were first in the exams."

"So I was. But nobody makes it tae sergeant in under eight years."

"So Paul will hae a long wait an all?"

"Naw, Auntie. There's big changes coming and he'll go into the CID. Me? I just love being in uniform and out in the community. Like last night. Listen to this," said Sam, who was now aware that Rachel needed some cheering up. "Pimpernel Pete and me were chumming each other down by the back door o Crawford's."

"The whisky bond or the biscuits?"

"Carrie! Just hold yer wheesht and listen. And it's the biscuit factory. There we were, guarding each other's poke o chips, when we saw the back door into the biscuit factory was standing wide open. Hello! Hello! we thought. And we were right – for inside, sprawling on the floor, was a sailor. His language wasn't English but there was no mistaking what he was saying an doing to the clapped-out auld hoor he was with . . ."

"Sam," exclaimed Rachel, "that's maybe the only way the poor woman can earn her crust."

"She was short-changing him," continued Sam defensively. "So the Pimpernel, who'd finished his chips afore me, asked what the problem was. Soon, out from the shadows comes Foxy Freddie, the nightshift labourer, who says his wife wasn't keeping very well, so every night (at his break-time he swore to us) he nips out the back door and goes over the Links back into Halmyre Street, runs up the three flights o stairs to check the bairns are all in bed and sleeping, then runs back down the stairs, up Halmyre Street, over the Links and raps three times sharply on the back door at exactly twenty-five minutes after he left and John Campbell here lets him in. 'That right?' says the Pimpernel looking over at John Campbell who's busy trying to hide a bogey loaded up with tins o biscuits, shortbread, Viennese Whirls, big dollops o butter and uncooked shortbread."

"They'd be at the lash," interrupted Bella.

"Aye, they were. But listen. Freddie then says that, after he'd been gone only twenty minutes, was there no a frantic knocking on the door? Johnny, thinking there must have been something awful wrong at Freddie's house, flings open the door and – lo and behold! – Elsie the hoor – sorry, Mammy – the working lady o the night and her punter both faw in. Well, the lassie gets such a wallop she cannae go on because there's more than her dignity been hurt and the wee sailor's no for going on either as he cannae perform to a live audience. Sae the twa o them are now rolling about the flair, him trying to find out where she keeps her money and her screaming that a contract, though verbal, was binding. I've now finished my chips so I steps in to help the Pimpernel separate them and haul them to their feet. 'Right,' says Pimpernel Pete, 'How much did you charge him?' 'A fiver,' she replies as she produces the note and hands it to Pete. 'Hold on,' says Pete as the wee sailor goes to grab the note from his hand. 'I think the solution is' – and here he tells me out o the side o his mouth that we dinnae want to charge them and have all that paper work – 'that we divvie the fiver atween ye baith.' Nobody's got change of a fiver but by doing a whip-round we gather up enough for Captain Cook and syne Pete tells Elsie she'll get her share when he sees her in the Kings Wark pub the morn's night."

"So all's well that ends well?" spluttered Carrie who was now in a fit of giggles.

"No. Ye see, after Romeo and Juliet depart, Pete turns his attention to the bogey and asks, 'What have we got here then?' 'Just some raffle prizes for the Works dance on Friday,' quips Freddie as he tries to push the lumps of butter and uncooked shortbread out of sight."

"But why would they want uncooked shortbread?" interposed Bella.

"Evidently it makes brilliant crumble," responded Sam before continuing his story. " 'That's right,' says Pete and tosses Freddie a couple o bob, announcing, 'An' I've just bought the first six winning tickets.' Then he goes over to the bogey and lifts six tins o shortbread."

Sam bent down and out of a carrier-bag produced two tins of shortbread and said with a grin: "Know this? He sent one to you, Mammy, and one to you, Auntie Bella."

"Oh, thanks a million, Sam. And such a bonnie tartan tin," declared Bella. "But here, son, next time you're in Crawford's, just you mind, I wouldn't half like trying the crumble stuff!"

9

AN ISLAND BREAK

Rachel felt truly like a queen as Sam steered his brand new Morris shooting-brake along the winding road. They were off to Mallaig to catch the ferry for the Outer Isles and the car was laden with everything she'd collected for Hannah and her increasingly large brood. She normally went by train to Mallaig but there was a limit to what she could carry, so when Sam said how much he would like a trip to the Hebrides to see Hannah, his mother had jumped at the chance.

She generally didn't pay much attention to the scenery as her thoughts would dwell on Hannah and how she was managing – but today, sitting beside Sam in the front seat of the car, she was able to agree that Scotland was indeed a beautiful country. They'd stopped briefly in Callander to have some tea and a sandwich and now they were on their way to Tyndrum by way of bonnie Strathyre and even more breathtaking Lochearnhead where all you could do was wonder at the beauty of the rivers, lochs and mountains. They continued on to Bridge of Orchy and then tackled the steep climb up to the Black Mount. It was here that Sam had insisted on stopping to admire the view down to Loch Tulla which they'd just skirted. "D'ye know this is one o the best views in the whole o Scotland?"

Rachel silently agreed but her thoughts were carrying her beyond that scene and into the next part of their journey: to Rannoch Moor and Glencoe. Every time that Rachel passed through these glens it had been raining and the hills that rose steeply on either side seemed to loom so closely that she felt as though she were being trapped. The thought of all the betrayal and misery linked to those places lay like a dead weight upon her. She dearly hoped there was no truth in the ghost story of that MacDonald woman who had seen her husband slain by the treacherous Campbells and who had then been chased with her two infants far out into the open spaces where they had slowly died of hunger and exposure. It was still believed that she haunted those glens, waiting to entice a Campbell into the bleak moors where she would watch him die, as she and her children had, away back on that chill February in 1692.

"Penny for them?" asked Sam, intrigued by his mother's mystical stare.

'Oh, I've just been looking down into these glens that I hope – with a bit of luck – we'll soon be whizzing through." She paused for several minutes. "Sam," she pleaded, "please don't stop now until we reach Ballachulish."

"Eh?"

"Look, Sam, just you drive as fast as you can and stop for no one."

Sam laughed loudly. "Och, Mam, surely ye don't believe that auld ghost story about the MacDonald woman. And let's face it: I'm related through my father tae the Campbells and he's from the conshie-objector side o the family, so she can hardly blame me for the Glencoe massacre."

Rachel shivered. "See, the weather's closing in. Let's just get going." She walked over to the car and settled herself in. It had been good to hear Sam laugh. The last few weeks must have been so hard for him but he'd said nothing. And it was all because both he and Paul, with their ordinary promotion exams behind them, had gone on to sit the accelerated police promotion exams. Both had done very well in the written submissions – especially Sam, who had come third in the whole of Scotland. However, it was when they had to be interviewed by the panel made up of a psychologist, five senior officers selected from various Scottish Police Forces and a chairman who was none other than Edinburgh's Chief Constable that things grew difficult for Sam. Asked which rank he imagined he might end up with, he had replied in his typically blunt way that, as he was still waiting to fill dead man's shoes at sergeant level, which could take up to another five years, finally being promoted to inspector would seem reasonable.

Paul's answer to the same question was, "No matter which rung on the ladder I'm on, I'll always be aiming for the next one." Naturally enough, Paul's answer was far better in the panel's eyes and so he became one of the twelve young men selected out of the four hundred who had applied for accelerated promotion. The other thing that still stuck in Sam's throat was that, out of those twelve selected for stardom (as he saw it) six were from Edinburgh and not one, including Paul, had matched his own marks in the written exam!

Rachel vowed there and then that she would try to talk about that with Sam just as soon as they were clear of Glencoe. Suddenly she was jolted out of her thoughts when Sam announced, "That's us through Glencoe and I never got one invitation frae a lassie to go for a dander on the moor."

"You mean the Ballachulish ferry is within spitting distance at long last?"

"Well, a couple o miles further on I suppose you could do it."

Rachel relaxed in her seat. She knew it was crazy to believe in ghost stories but you never could be absolutely sure, could you?

It was as they were merrily buzzing along by the banks of Loch Linnhe on their way to Fort William and from there on to Mallaig that Rachel decided that the time was right to speak to her laddie. "Sam," she began confidentially, "about what happened at the accelerated . . ."

"Just leave it be, Mam."

"Well, I can't. Especially now that Paul will make it to sergeant before you."

"No he won't."

"But he'll be a sergeant just as soon as he finishes his year's special training at Tulliallan College!"

"Naw. You see, as a sop . . ."

"Sop?" Rachel interrupted.

"Aye, a bribe that is to hide the fact I came first in the exams in Edinburgh and then, to add insult to injury, they allowed a bloody blinkered psychologist, who was probably born with a silver spoon in his mouth, to decide that I'm no senior officer material!"

"So what exactly is this – sop?"

"Just promoted me to sergeant, they have."

Rachel gasped incredulously and her melancholy expression switched suddenly to an expansive grin. "They have?"

"Aye. I start in Gayfield – well, the Drylaw section of B Division – next week."

"Oh that's absolutely wonderful. And I know you'll make a good job of it."

Sam smiled wryly. "Maybe aye; maybe no. You see, Pimpernel Pete has blotted his copybook again and he's being transferred out o Leith to get him away from his demon drinking dens."

"Don't tell me he's being transferred to Drylaw and on to *your* shift."

"Where else? Thinking o getting him to start up Community Involvement, they are." Sam turned to wink at his mother. "Now," he continued with a chuckle, "Pete's interpretation o Community Involvement might not be exactly what the powers that be want – know what I mean?"

When the ferry eventually docked at Lochboisdale, Sam was standing at the rail gazing down at the crowd of folk on the quay. No mistaking it – that was their Jamie waiting for them. "Thank goodness!" Sam murmured to himself. Unloading the contents of his shooting-brake at Mallaig and stowing all the cargo bound for Hannah had taken fifteen trips. It had taken so long indeed that he nearly didn't have time to park the car safely behind the fish market before jumping aboard the boat. Then he'd settled down to enjoy the journey. Apart from his Far East cruise to Korea, courtesy of Her Majesty's government, and his trips to play football in England and Wales for the Edinburgh Police, Sam had never travelled far. He didn't even have a passport – you didn't need one to go from Restalrig to Portobello for a paddle in the Firth of Forth whenever the sun put in an appearance. But as the ferry gently ploughed its way westward, Sam had been quite overawed by the sheer beauty of the Hebrides. Tiny islands glistened in the turquoise sea: beyond them lay the rounded hills – and he felt a sense of calm serenity as the magnificence of the view seeped into his bones.

"Let's be going, Sam," urged Rachel as she grabbed a laden bag and began to make her way to the gangplank. Sam was about to follow her when he realised that Jamie was now on board and bounding towards them, both hands outstretched in welcome.

Sam eagerly shook Jamie's hand. "Great that you could come to meet us," he said, gesturing meaningfully towards their mountain of baggage.

"Got the kitchen sink and all?"

"You saying that you're actually due to be linked up to the water system?" asked Rachel, unable to keep her excitement in check.

"No. Not this year but they do say it'll begin to happen next year and we should all be flushing away happily by 1966." Rachel's enthusiasm faded before Jamie quickly added, "But having the electricity has made all the difference. And it's only been cut off a couple of times in the last three months."

"Forget to pay your bill, did you?" asked Sam.

"No, no," said Rachel reprovingly. "The wind would have done that. Just wait till you feel how strong it blows hereabouts."

Sam felt a catch in his throat as soon as he entered the croft house. There was his sister, Hannah, surrounded by her happy brood, pregnant as ever but oozing contentment. Seven in all she had now, two of whom were trying to hide behind their mother's back, unsure who this unfamiliar and very tall stranger might be. As Sam drew Hannah close in a loving embrace, the children took refuge around Rachel, their Granny, eager to discover what treasures she had brought. "Now," said Sam firmly, as he let Hannah go, "I'm here for ten days and I want to be of some use. So are there any chores you'd like me to do?"

Hannah and Rachel both laughed aloud. "Well," Hannah began, "the coal was delivered this morning."

"So?"

"They just tip it out at the bottom of the hill and we have to barrow it up in the old pram."

"Are you saying there's more than two bags to be brought up?"

"Two hundredweight?" exclaimed Hannah. "Oh no, we only get a delivery twice a year – so it's four tons at a time."

Sam walked over to the window to remind himself just how steep the brae was and shrugged stoically. "Suppose it'll take quite a few trips?"

"Aye," added Jamie. "But, you see, every time someone goes out they wheel the pram to the bottom of the hill and the next person to be coming back fills the pram up and pushes it back up the hill."

"D'ye think we'll have it all up by the time I leave?"

"Of course," replied Hannah.

"Maybe not," interrupted Jamie. "Remember we're to have a couple of days going over to cut the peat and Sam could help at that too."

"Cut the peat?"

"Aye, over on yon wee island. Best peat you can get is over there. We all go. Make a day out of it."

"And we take a picnic," broke in Morag, who was desperate to get in on the conversation.

Sam smiled. "I'm thinking I'll be fully occupied this holiday."

"You certainly will," replied Hannah, "because if you've any spare time it would be great if you could start to dig out the drains for when the water arrives!"

Sam and Hannah were still sitting at the table, quite unaware that Jamie and Rachel had seen to the washing and bedding of the children. Hannah was just so hungry for news of home and of all the folk she knew there.

"So Paul's courting, is he?"

"Aye," replied Sam. "A Newhaven lassie."

"A bow-tow?"

"Well I suppose you might call her a bow-tow as her dad's a fisherman. But she's been educated at Gillespie's Ladies College no less. She's at Moray House now, training to be a teacher."

"And she's fancying our Paul?"

"Aye. Especially now he's got the chance o ending up as a big cheese."

Hannah didn't answer – she was surprised that Sam had alluded to Paul being on the accelerated promotion course as Rachel had told her in strict confidence that Sam was a bit bruised by the whole affair.

"Mind you," Sam continued, "it'll still take him a fair while tae live down all his first cock-ups on the job."

"Like what?"

"Well on his very first week at Craigmillar, Paul was put under the wing o the big sergeant, Jock Ferguson, and at midnight on his first shift there they were, chasing after two thieves who'd grabbed the takings out o the hand o the barman in the Last Stand pub just as he was about to put them in the night safe. Anyway, being on the spot, they took after them and big Jock tackles one to the ground. Unfortunately he was no the one with the money, Jock then grabs the man by the throat and asks who his accomplice is. When no answer's forthcoming Jock says, 'Right, unless you give me his name I am gonnae send my constable here to get a big pail of shite and when he comes back with it I'm going to put your heid in it until ye mind your pal's name.' But isn't the feet cawed frae Jock when Paul asks, 'But, Sergeant, where'll I get a pail of excrement at this time of night?' "

Hannah laughed. "Oh Sam, isn't that just like Paul?"

"Aye, and then when he was allowed out on his own, wasn't he on night shift! As per usual, he's constipated and taken a big doze o Syrup of Figs, which results in him having an urgent call of nature at midnight. So as all the usual haunts the police can depend on to allow them the use of their lavvies are closed, doesn't he just decide to relieve himself on a paper in the police box at Balgreen?"

"Aren't there toilet facilities in the police boxes?"

"Naw Hannah, there's no. So, Paul being our Paul, he has the *Evening News* all spread out on the floor and he's just got himself perched over it when a runaway lorry careers down the hill on Gorgie Road, and wallops the police box a great hefty glancing blow. Slowly but surely the box collapses into four sections and there's our Paul exposed to the all the world with his trousers at his feet and still hunched over the paper."

Hannah tried hard not to laugh but couldn't help tittering as she visualised the graphic scene. "But Sam," she eventually managed to say, "he could have been killed. I mean the awful fright he must have got!"

"Fright? I suppose so but – know something? – he hasn't been constipated ever since!" Sam sniggered as he rose and went over to his bag and brought out a paper parcel which he handed to Hannah. "Went into a bookshop and got you these."

Hannah unwrapped the two books. "That was very kind of you, Sam."

Sam shrugged. "Well, I remembered how much you loved books. Your nose was never out o them." He turned and looked about the room that was liberally decorated with piles of washing, ironing and dirty dishes, and heaved a sigh. "Don't know when ye'll get the time to read them though?"

Hannah went over and put her arms around his neck, "I'll keep them for when I go to the hospital in Daliburgh. The nuns always take me in two weeks before I'm due, to give me a rest. A good book puts the time in just fine. Now you've brought me up to date on Paul and I got a letter from Alice last week. So now I only have to find out what Carrie's up to."

"She's moving house the morn," Sam informed her. Just then the wind began to howl around the croft house. "Would you listen to that gale! And here was me thinking that all they stories Mammy told me about the storms up here were just fairy tales."

He and Hannah walked over to the window from where they could plainly view the sea being whipped into a frenzy.

"See when Jamie and his step-brothers are out fishing at night and a storm like this gets up? I can't sleep. I try hard not to remember the sinking of the Margaret Paton and I just pray that nothing like that ever happens here."

"Aye," whispered Sam, "It's gone on thirteen years – maybe fourteen – since the Margaret Paton went down. Hogmanay of 1949 it was when she should have come back to Newhaven." Sam huffed derisively, "But you know? It wasn't until the fifth of January when she was six days over-due that they sent out an RAF plane to search the Coral Reef in the North Sea."

"Right enough, Sam, that was where she was last seen but they found nothing. No. All thirteen of the crew and their boat were gone forever!" Shaking her head Hannah paused. "And do you remember how you *insisted* that

Carrie and I went with you to the service in the Newhaven kirk? We had to stand out in the street, we did. Aye, the whole of Newhaven, Leith and Granton had turned out to pay their respects. All those communities were completely devastated by that terrible disaster. Even our Daddy was there, Sam, but he didn't seem to notice us."

"Aye, but we hadn't come there to see *him*. It was because when I was a wee laddie and trying to keep us all thegither the trawlermen were aye so guid at giving me a pauckle o fish. I minded on that and just *had* to pay my respects to the men who'd aw been lost. *And* I needed you and Carrie tae chum me to the memorial service."

Sister and brother sat silently for what seemed an age, each with their own memories of that awful event.

In no time at all, so it seemed to everyone, the peat had been dug and the coal safely transported up to the croft. Reluctantly, Rachel and Sam made preparations for their return home from the Isles. Hannah pressed them to take some of her fresh eggs but Rachel smilingly declined, saying they'd be sure to get smashed one way or another on the long journey back. The true reason, however, was that the island hens were all fed on herring. That was fine if one didn't mind a herring-flavoured boiled egg – but Rachel's discerning palate knew that the fishy flavour did little for fruit scones and even less for a fruit cake!

In Leith meanwhile, Carrie and Will were busily settling into their new home, with which they were all delighted. In the kitchen, Will was preparing sandwiches for lunch while Donald was outside furiously digging what would become a vegetable plot. Not even the twelve pounds a month mortgage payment had put Carrie off. And to add to this financial burden Sophie was now a junior pupil at Leith Academy where the annual fee was a hefty twelve pounds. So a little extra income would be welcome, she felt.

After lunch, Carrie decided to walk along by Hermitage Park to buy a few groceries at the Leith Provident Co-operative. This done, she emerged from the shop to find it was now raining hard – but after all it was April so what else could one expect? Much less expected was the sight of a small, dishevelled and totally drenched man hovering at the school gates. He looked so comical that Carrie could hardly stop herself laughing out loud. His trouser legs were obviously not on speaking terms with his feet since they were a good three inches above his ankles, while his scruffy shoes squelched loudly as he paced up and down. His well-worn brown suit was shiny and decidedly greasy but it was his shirt that really amazed her. Once crisp and white no doubt, it was now liberally bespeckled with what could only be spots of blood (Carrie hoped these came only from a care-less shave and nothing worse) while the turned-up collar edges looked as if they'd been placed in dinky curlers all night.

"Can I help you at all?" Carrie found herself asking this distraught personage.

"I can't say. You see, I'm the headmaster here and I'm looking for a secretary."

"Is she late?"

"Well, she's certainly my *late* secretary but she's not late for work. She's left me in the lurch. I have a *most* important letter that *must* go in the post today, so I've decided to wait here on the off-chance that the good Lord will providen-tially send me another secretary."

Carrie hesitated. The man's behaviour was even weirder than his dress, Who, in his right mind, she wondered, would expect to find a school secretary walking along a quiet back street looking for a job? But maybe he wasn't entirely mad. After all, hadn't she herself been a competent secretary to that unorthodox character, Jock Elmslie, at the Roperie? Almost involuntarily, she found herself saying, "I can type. Could I be of any use to you?"

The man's hands flew above his head and he exclaimed, "I just *knew* God wouldn't let me down and that he'd send me help before the Committee makes its final decision."

"Well," said Carrie, "Just let me go home first to tell my family. Then I'll come back and do what I can to be of assistance to you."

Some hours later, when Carrie entered the headmaster's study, she was surprised to discover it hadn't changed in the slightest since she herself had been a pupil there. The head's desk dominated the room and in one corner stood a table furnished with an Imperial typewriter and telephone. Once seated at his desk the headmaster introduced himself. "I am Mr Hamish Brand, headmaster here, and I require you to type this draft letter *exactly* as I have written it." Carrie set to work but was puzzled. The letter was addressed to the Director of Education. Why, she wondered, did Mr Brand imagine he could question a decision of the Director? And should he be sending a letter that states: "I have been headmaster at Hermitage Park School for the past twelve years and have three more years before reaching retirement age. Surely it would be appropriate for me to be promoted at this stage to one of our more prestigious places of education, while the existing head teacher there would be transferred to

Hermitage Park, where there would be many valuable opportunities to gain experience in dealing with working class children and their parents, who are such a burden on society."

By the time Carrie had finished typing she was red with rage and indignation. This man was an utter snob. Didn't he realise that most of the children who attended Hermitage Park went on to become useful members of the community and were a burden to no one?

Mr Brand read the typed letter through, with frequent nods of approval – less, Carrie felt, for the quality of her typing than for the self-evident justice of his own case for promotion. His unmistakable talents had been overlooked for far too long! Carrie had begun typing the envelope when a middle-aged teacher burst into the room.

"Headmaster, oh, Headmaster!" he cried out. "Little Alice Doig has just swallowed a piece of chalk!"

"And what colour was the chalk, Mr Jamieson?" demanded Mr Brand.

"I don't know I'm sure, sir," came the reply.

Carrie meanwhile had run into the corridor to aid the choking child. After two well-placed thumps on Alice's back the chalk few out of her mouth. Cradling the weeping girl to her chest, she wondered again about this man Brand, but was still more flummoxed when he contemptuously picked up the piece of chalk, handed it to Mr Jamieson and advised him to wash it thoroughly.

"This coloured chalk is twice the cost of white so please do not let this kind of incident recur. And kindly employ this yellow chalk in an object-lesson to the class on how *not* to choke oneself."

Brand then turned his attention to Carrie. "I am pleased to offer you the post of school secretary with immediate effect and your hours will be made convenient, if practicable, for your own domestic arrangements."

The offer seemed ideal, despite her serious misgivings about Brand's character. Almost without hesitation, Carrie accepted. Some extra money coming into the household would make life a lot easier for them all.

10
A TRIO OF MISHAPS

Newly appointed Inspector Paul Campbell was making his way down the High Street when he became aware of a police constable chasing after two small boys and shouting "Stop these wee thieves!" to the passers-by, who were naturally refusing to get involved. Paul quickly slipped into narrow Anchor Close and, just as the boys were about to run past the entry, he shouted, "Quick! In here. The polis . . ."

"Where, where?" demanded the two in unison.

"Here," called Paul, grabbing both lads by the collar.

While the boys wriggled to free themselves, the constable had also reached Anchor Close and promptly relieved Paul of the smaller of the two scallywags.

"I've chased these laddies all the way from Princes Street, so I have," the breathless constable explained. "And just how I'm going to get them down to Gayfield Square, I simply don't know."

"No transport then?"

"There is, but it's down on Rose Street and it's already overloaded with half the country shoplifting."

Paul smiled. He well understood how frustrated the young man felt. Shoplifting was a nightmare at Christmas. And it wasn't only the known thieves. No, Christmas seemed to be a time when it was acceptable for anyone, from any walk of life, to ease the financial pressures of Christmas by not paying for some of their purchases. "Look," he said to the constable, "I'm going down that way to interview a witness, so how about we each hold on to one of 'em." Paul then looked at the children before asking, "Are they old enough to be charged?"

The constable shook his head. "No. But for the last three Saturdays they've been stealing to order and our inspector insists that we run them in and send for their parents."

"And how long does it take for the parents to put in an appearance?"

The constable would like to have said, "Bloody hours!" but tempered his language. "Well, last week they didn't turn up till nine o'clock – which meant we had to feed the wee blighters."

"An' this week," the cockier of the two piped up, "when you go up to the Deep Sea for our chips, I'm wantin a hale fish with mine no a dried up old white pudden!"

When they reached Gayfield Square, Paul thought the station resembled a World War One field hospital rather than a police station. Shoplifters mingled with both the walking wounded and the drunks, while one very drunk driver, who had been taken in for his own safety, was swaying precariously and demanding loudly if the station sergeant knew who he was.

"Not really," the sergeant coolly replied. "But when the woman we think may be your wife turns up she might know." His attention now turned to the two young boys and he gave a groan on instantly recognising them. "Not you two again!" The two lads seemed quite unfazed as the sergeant signalled to the constable to put them into safe custody.

"Shall I lock them in one of the downstairs cells?"

"Aye, you do that," agreed the sergeant.

"But, sergeant, I am well aware I have no authority here," Paul intervened, "but I must insist that you do not lock up, in a windowless cell, two young boys who are under the age of responsibility."

The sergeant was about to argue strenuously but, aware that Paul one day might well be the senior officer at Gayfield and that he himself still had ten years to serve before his pension would come along, decided that compromise might be the best option. "Okay, sir, but the only other place we can hold them is in the interview office behind me.

This arrangement was not to the constable's liking. "Look, sarge," he exclaimed, "you know they two are a right pair of Houdinis."

The sergeant nodded. "I know that. But look," and he gestured around the room. "If this isn't enough to be going on with, Drylaw's wanting assistance from us and are also demanding the use of our van!"

By now Paul had taken stock of the general mayhem in the room. "Surely you mean that *you* need Drylaw's assistance?"

The sergeant shook his head with mock gravity. "No, sir. Seems my opposite number over there in Drylaw thinks he's a sub-mariner!"

"Are you saying my brother Sam's in deep water?"

Not only did the sergeant nod wisely but so did all the other officers.

Sam was being driven around Drylaw subdivision in the patrol van by a constable on their way towards Cramond foreshore to meet up with Pimpernel Pete. The first thing that caught Sam's eye was Pete running along by the water's edge, frantically signalling to the two mounted police officers who were exercising their horses offshore while seeming quite unaware that they were driving the animals towards the quicksand! They seemed oblivious moreover to the fact that the tide had turned and, as was usual in the Firth of Forth, was now racing back in.

As the van drew level with Pete, the Pimpernel shouted, "Would you credit it? Twa idiots like them being in charge of beasts that have more savvy than they have!"

Sam nodded. "Just leave them be. They probably think they're much too superior to listen to us."

Pete jumped into the van. "But the poor horses . . ."

Sam jumped from the van. "Right enough," he agreed, walking to the water's edge and finding that one of the horses had become embedded in the sand and that the other seemed to be going to its rescue. Without hesitation, Sam placed his hands around his mouth and called out, "Don't try to rescue your pal!" His warning came too late, however, or went unheeded, because the second rider was now in position to grab the reins of the trapped horse in an effort to pull it free. After three fruitless attempts, he quickly let go of the reins, realising that he too was now sinking fast into the quicksand.

Sam turned to Pete who had joined him at the water's edge and, pointing to the marooned pair of riders, remarked caustically, "I thought you needed some sort of common-sense to get into the mounted division – so how in the devil's name did these twa get in?" Pete laughed as Sam started to shout, "Get your backsides out of they saddles. Don't you blinking idiots realise your weight is keeping them trapped?" The mounted officers made no response, so Sam went on: "Once these poor beasts have only them-selves to look after, they'll start to swim . . ."

One of the mounties, who by now had the sense to judge what a pickle they were in, interrupted Sam by shouting back, "If we dismount, our riding boots will get soaked."

Standing up in the stirrups, he pointed to the waters swirling and gushing around the horses' legs.

Turning to Pete, Sam ordered, "Quick! Take the van and drive out towards them."

"But sarge, will the van no sink tae?"

Sam sighed in exasperation. "Only if you drive out too far. Oh, and look in the back of the van for a rope, Pete."

As soon as the van had been driven as near to the horses as they judged safe, Sam and Pete leapt out. First, they tied the rope firmly round the front bumper of the van and then paddled over to the first horse and handed the other end of the rope to its rider. "Now, seeing you don't want to get your feet wet," instructed Sam brusquely, "when the van goes into reverse and I go round to the beast's rear to push, you urge the animal forward."

The idea seemed sound enough; but as the van driver tried to reverse it was evident that he couldn't – the tide having now brought the water half way up the wheels!

All four officers looked on aghast as the water began rushing into the van. Thereupon, deciding that getting their boots wet was the wiser option, the two mounted officers jumped from their horses and splashed into the water.

"Can't think what'll happen when we confess we let two of the best horses in the Edinburgh stables drown," said one of them as he and his mate began paddling towards the shoreline. They needn't have worried, however, because with their weight off the horses' backs, along with the buoyancy of the water, the beasts quickly freed themselves and could be seen swimming and then galloping towards the dry land.

The van, however, proved to be well and truly stuck even with its load lightened. Pete took the driver's place so that he could try his luck at reversing the vehicle out of danger – but that didn't help either. Sam, using all his native tenacity, attempted to push it to safety with his backside but only succeeded in losing his balance and tumbling into the water, from where he was forced to watch in mounting dismay as his hitherto immaculate cap floated away.

"Any ideas on what we should do now?" Pete yelled out of the van's window.

Sam, by now feeling the distinct chill of the waist-high water, raised both hands in a gesture of despair and gave the only appropriate order in the circumstances: "Abandon ship!"

On reaching the shore, wet and bedraggled, they were not in the least surprised to discover that their mounted colleagues had ridden off into the sunset, leaving the hapless trio to explain how their now almost totally submerged van had become a submarine.

Pete (being Pete) felt that they should all stand to attention and salute the van as it disappeared beneath the waves. Their driver, being the only one still in possession of a dry whistle, put it to his lips and blew a final tribute to the van.

"You know," Pete observed, "when the tide goes out again tomorrow they'll easily haul the van out. The only problem is – it'll be a complete write-off."

"Aye," agreed Sam ruefully, "along with my corn beef sandwiches. No to mention the prospects of me being made up to inspector in the next two years!"

As the sergeant finished giving Paul a graphic account of the van's mishap, he did try valiantly to check his laughter, but in the end could only apologise and say, "Sorry. But you have to admit, inspector, it was a truly titanic disaster!"

Paul said nothing. He knew he hadn't the divisional authority to censure the sergeant's amusement so he abruptly turned on his heel and made for the door. He had just turned into Gayfield Square when he became aware that one of the detained boys had just jumped out of the interview room window and was urging his friend to do likewise.

"Ah wid, but ah'm feart," the young lad replied, now hanging from the windowsill by his fingertips.

Paul tore back into the station and shouted to the station sergeant, while pointing to the closed door of the interview room, "These two wee varmints are escaping. One has got out of the window and the other is just about to kill himself when he jumps."

The sergeant's face turned ashen. "B-b-but," he spluttered, "that's the worst thing you can do in the force!"

"The *very* worst thing," endorsed Paul emphatically. "To lose a prisoner! And the powers that be won't care if they're eight years old or eighty! Now, I'm going after them because you and I will be in even deeper water than my brother if we don't get them back."

Paul was already halfway out of the office when the sergeant hollered, "What can I do?"

"Get the flashers going on the top of the boxes and tell everyone to be on the lookout for our van and when you get contact with it tell the occupants . . ."

"The driver and your brother."

"To catch up with me somewhere in London Street."

The two little lads had a good head start on him but Paul, like Sam, was athletic, and much to the boys' dismay, they could see that his fast strides were gaining on them. They had turned out of Gayfield Square into London Street and couldn't believe their luck when they came across a wood yard into which they quickly escaped. Paul came round the corner just in time to see where they would be hiding. Reaching the gate to the yard, Paul was faced with a dilemma. Should he go into the yard and risk allowing the tearaways to escape again through the unguarded gate? Or should he stay at the entrance and await assistance. He decided his best bet was to wait quietly at the gate.

Thirty minutes had passed before the van came into view. Thirty minutes during which he had listened as the boys shifted themselves from one pile of wood to another. Once he even saw them peering out to see if the coast was clear.

As soon as the van drew up at the entrance to the wood yard, Paul signed to Sam and his driver to keep as quiet as possible. Then he sidled over to the van and carefully outlined his plan. Suddenly, the van's engine revved up and the driver reversed some distance along the street before screeching forward as fast and as noisily possible. Both Sam and the driver then jumped out, making sure to bang the doors loudly.

"Great, you've made it! What kept you?" Paul shouted.

"Just picking up the big dogs," replied Sam loudly.

"Which of your hounds are on duty today?" Paul asked, winking at Sam.

"Yon dangerous Rottweiler and the massive German Shepherd that can tear a man to shreds in two minutes!" was Sam's instant rejoinder, as he opened the back door of the van and then loudly banged it shut. Silently, he signalled that, on a count of three, they should all act in unison by uttering a series of blood-curdling howls and menacing growls.

Without further ado the two young lads emerged from behind a stack of timber, one with both hands high in the air and the other frantically clutching the front of his trousers. "Okay, mister, we surrender," the first boy announced.

"Aye, so we dae," agreed the other. "I'm that feart, I'm aboot tae pee mysel!"

School was taking up after the Christmas holidays and Carrie was so excited. This would be the very last term she would have to put up with Mr Brand before he retired. He had sent a letter to the Director of Education offering to stay on for a further year but the blunt reply made it clear that the Director wouldn't wish him to remain for even one more term. In fact, since they had now filled his post, he could leave whenever he wished.

Carrie felt this information should alert Mr Brand to the fact that his unorthodox methods of running a school were no longer acceptable. She cringed, remembering how, on the very day they were closing for the Christmas holidays, the children had tumbled out of school and one little girl had been so anxious to escape that she'd run straight out into the road. The local store manager was driving along in his small Co-op van and collided with the child who had landed on the van's bonnet before rolling off and bouncing on the road.

The distraught man had rushed into school to report the accident and was accosted by Mr Brand who demanded to know what the panic was all about. Pulling at the headmaster's coat sleeve, the driver gasped, "Oh, sir! I've just knocked down one of your pupils. A wee lassie."

"Do you know her name?"

"Aye," replied the man, "It's wee Primrose Shepherd."

"There, there," replied Brand, fussily removing the man's hand from his arm, "Don't go upsetting yourself. Primrose wasn't one of our brighter pupils . . ."

With a screech of horror, the man fled from the school before Carrie or anyone else could explain that Mr Brand had a distinct inability to finish sentences adequately and was equally incapable of giving a clear explanation. In the case of poor Primrose, one might have expected him to continue, ". . . and so she is very apt to run on to the road without looking."

The ringing of the school bell had Carrie wondering where the headmaster had gone. On a Monday, as distinct from any other weekday, Brand was generally early, hoping to catch members of his staff arriving at the last moment. Today, however, there was a surprise visit by two inspectors that had caught everyone napping. At first they had gone to the Head's office, but in his absence had made their way along to the Infants' Mistress's room. Already on duty, as ever, Miss Wright was about to go out and bring the infants in from the playground. On seeing the inspectors, however, she asked if she might be of help.

"Yes indeed," the senior officer replied. "We've just popped in to see you since we hear that you are willing to try out the Initial Teaching Alphabet here?"

Miss Wright preened herself. She was one of the few teachers who were sold on this novel teaching method and she was more than pleased to ask both gentlemen to sit down and discuss its merits

It was nearly nine-thirty when the headmaster's car at last drew up at the school gates and the janitor ran to warn Mr Brand of the surprise visit from the inspectors. The headmaster bounded up the steps, flinging his battered old briefcase into the rubbish collection area before charging through the corridors. As nonchalantly as possible he then paced up and down until the inspectors eventually emerged from Miss Wright's room."

"A beautiful morning, gentlemen!" exclaimed Mr Brand, extending his hand to wish both men a Happy New Year. "I'm so sorry I missed you when you arrived but I've just been going around the school wishing my staff the compliments of the season."

Neither man was in the least fooled by Mr Brand. They knew him of old – only too well – and the head was further put out when they firmly declined to join him in his office for a cup of tea.

Mr Brand was muttering to himself as he looked in the mirror and combed his hair. "Carrie," he murmured smoothly, "to look at me you wouldn't think I'd soon be retiring, would you?"

Carrie declined to answer and continued with her work, knowing full well that this would be a prelude to a lengthy sob-story about how his wife didn't understand him. Carrie was fully prepared to accept that complaint – because neither she nor or anyone else at the school understood him either! And what riled most of all was that on Monday mornings he would bestow a tuppenny Polo mint on whichever member of staff he thought could be persuaded to understand him.

He had only just turned from the mirror and surreptitiously placed a Polo tube beside Carrie's typewriter when a sudden commotion in the corridor had him dashing to shut his office door. Too late! The store manager had successfully stuck a foot in the door and pushed it open with a ferocious wallop of his left fist as he hauled little Davie Scott inside with his right arm.

"Whatever is the meaning of this disgraceful fracas?" fumed Mr Brand.

Shaking Davie by the scruff of the neck, the store manager bellowed, "This wee blighter has just stolen a packet of effing crisps." He then conceded to the bewildered Headmaster, "Okay, so we're self-service now, but that doesn't mean folk helping themselves without paying."

"Quite so," agreed Mr Brand suavely. Taking the packet of crisps from the store manager's hand, he proceeded to open it and extract a crisp, which he popped into his mouth before explaining to Carrie, "By the way, these are not Effing's Crisps at all; they are Smith's Ready-Salted." He turned back to the store manager. "So you're saying you caught this petty miscreant red-handed?"

The store manager sighed. "Ah just told ye, did ah no? And for all you ever do about onything, ah think I'll just go straight and get the polis."

This threat upset Mr Brand because, as Carrie well knew, he was (as her old Granny would have said) "not the clean tattie" and the last thing he would want was for the police to be brought into the matter. "Come, come now, my good fellow. Surely, you don't want to mar this young lad's life by giving him a criminal record?"

The store manager snorted.

"And I can assure you that, if you leave the matter with me, I will certainly deal with the boy more severely than the constabulary would." Mr Brand lifted the lid of his desk and brought out his Rainy Day tin from which he ostentatiously paid for the crisps. The store manager made to leave but turned back and advanced towards Davie while addressing the headmaster. "And you *will* belt this wee blighter good and hard?"

"That I shall indeed, my good fellow," Brand unctuously assured him as he made to usher the manager from his room. "Oh yes! My motto is: *spare the rod and spoil the child!*"

As soon as Mr Brand had stepped into the corridor, Carrie picked up the Polo tube and deposited it in the wastepaper basket. Then she became aware that young Davie was twisting, turning and clutching the back of his trousers. "Davie," she exclaimed, "whatever is the matter with you?"

"Oh, Mrs Fraser, I'm that feart of the belting he's gonnae give me, I'm nearly shitting myself."

"But Davie, how often do I have to tell you that stealing is wrong. And you could end up in an approved school."

"I ken. But I was that hungry. I've had naething to eat since yesterday dinnertime because Maw was pissed again. And that approved school place is no aw that bad, so ah'm telt. Nae only d'ye get a cooked dinner and tea but ye hae a bed all to yersel!"

"Davie, approved schools are for really bad boys. And you're not that." Bending down, Carrie picked up her handbag from which she produced a buttered roll. "Here, Davie," she said, "you can eat this while you're away to the lavatory. But promise me you'll come back."

"Are you saying you want me to come back for a leathering? Nae chance! I'm doing a runner."

"Look, you'll get over getting belted but if you do a runner you'll miss your dinner. And Davie, it's mince and tatties today, followed by lemon meringue pie!"

"But them's my favourites." Davie thought carefully before adding, "Naethin else for it then. I'll just hae tae thole the belt. But here, Mrs Fraser, could you no put in a guid word for me?"

"I *will* try. But remember, Davie, Mr Brand has his standards."

Davie winked at Carrie as he made for the door. "Aye, and we aw ken what they are. Charges us bairns tuppence to see a film. Tuppence that ends up in his own tail."

An hour had gone by before Mr Brand returned to his office. Miss Wright had been in three times to see him but he'd managed to elude her successfully each time. He still had Davie to deal with, however, and was preparing to take out his leather tawse when he heard the ominous clicking of Miss Wright's heels advancing towards his door. Gesturing to Carrie and grabbing Davie by the collar, he jumped into the large walk-in stationery cupboard that stood just next to the office.

"Don't tell me that man isn't back yet!" snapped the Infants' Mistress, but before Carrie could answer the interval bell rang and Miss Wright hurried off to supervise the exodus of her Infants into the playground.

No sooner had she gone than Mr Brand surreptitiously pushed open the cupboard door and poked his head out.

"Ah, she's gone. Good! Now for my well-earned tea-break."

"Is there no going to be a rammie then?" Davie almost sang. Brand turned sharply and grabbed him by the jumper. "Oh, look an see what you've gone an done now," whined Davie. "Ripped my jumper worse, so you hae. And that'll no please my Mammy – nor the polis. This is a Police-Aided Clothing Model, so it is."

Mr Brand immediately let Davie go but pushed him further into the cupboard, muttering, "Impudent, ungrateful upstart. Just you stay in that cupboard until I have time to deal with you." He then turned to Carrie. "Look, I've had such a traumatic morning that I desperately need to get into the fresh air."

On his departure, Carrie was alerted by the banging on the store cupboard door and Davie shouting, "It's dark in here! Mammy! Daddy! Save me. Somebody get the polis."

Immediately Carrie stood up, switched on the light and opened the cupboard door slightly. "Shhh, Davie," she whispered comfortingly. "You'll be perfectly safe in there."

"Will I? And what about the bogeymen?"

"Bogeymen? Don't talk rubbish. Look, I'll away and get you a bottle of milk."

The afternoon session had just begun. Davie had been released from the cupboard by Carrie so that he could have lunch in the dinner hall. Now he was back in the cupboard, sitting on a chair, and plaintively asking Carrie when she peered in, "Hoo much langer hae I got to stay in here?"

"Do try to be patient, Davie. Mr Brand has been called away on urgent business."

"We bairns aw ken he goes hunting around the second-hand shops in Leith Walk."

"That's so he can buy things on the cheap that we need here in the school."

Davie started to cackle. "Oh aye? Like last week when he came back with a mangle?"

"Well you never know when things like that may come in handy."

"Right enough. When he's finished mangling the bairns he could mebbe straighten . . ."

"That's quite enough, Davie. Now, did Mrs Brockie give you your dinner?"

Leaping out of the cupboard, Davie pretended to be eating furiously. "Aye. And she's a smasher. Gave me doubling helpins when I told here I was getting blootered this afternoon."

Carrie was about to respond when she looked out into the corridor and saw Mr Brand sprinting towards her. "Quick, Davie! Back in the cupboard."

It was too late. Mr Brand sprang into the office and hurtled himself towards the boy. "Forgot that I had still to deal with you," he snorted before indicating that Davie should stand in front of his desk. "Now, David Scott, you were caught stealing and no one is required to steal." Mr Brand raised a finger and pointed to the ceiling, "Our Father in heaven – does he not provide for our every need?" He fixed Davie with a stern glare. "Does he not?"

Davie considered the question carefully before replying, "Well, Him and the Means Test."

Carrie sighed. She knew that, by this time in the afternoon, any connection Mr Brand had with reality would have long gone so she was not in the least surprised when he ignored Davie's response and began to preach aloud. "Doth he not clothe the humble sparrow? If He would do that for a simple bird, David, how much more will He do for you?" Davie said nothing but just looked about the room despairingly. "And are you aware, David Scott, that every day I, *your illustrious Headmaster*, go down on bended knees and thank God for all He has bestowed on me. Now, my lad, can you think of just one thing *you* can thank God for?" Davie shrugged and looked over to Carrie who was frantically hoping he would answer. "Come away, boy, there must be *one* thing you can think of to thank God for."

Davie shifted from one foot to the other and Carrie thought just how hard that question was for him. He lived in a condemned room and kitchen in Primrose Street along with six other siblings and his drunken parents; and the only cooked meals he ever got were his free dinners here at the school.

Furious at Davie's inability to respond, Mr Brand lifted the lid of his desk and, bringing out the cruel belt, bellowed, "Right! Have you never heard your miserable, scrounging mother thank God?" Davie's face lightened. "Come on then! What does she thank Him for?"

"Wall's steak pie!"

Mr Brand sank down on his chair and buried his head in his hands before groaning, "Wall's Steak Pie. Now tell me, Carrie, where in the Holy Bible does it mention Wall's Steak Pie?"

"I don't think it does, sir. So would it not be better if I took Davie back to his class?"

"Yes, pluck him out of my sight. For the sight of him doth offend my eye!"

11
STORM AND STRESS

Hannah gazed unseeingly as she stood at the window which faced the school. One of the few things that she disliked, even hated, about life on Herrig was that now, in December, daylight didn't surface until after nine in the morning and darkness shrouded the island by half past three in the afternoon. However, all that was compensated for when at midsummer the sun chased away the dusk almost before it had time to settle.

Angus, her youngest fifteen-month-old son, was now pulling vigorously at her skirt and she bent to pick him up. "Ah," she said teasingly, "so you think you should still be the baby? Well, that's Ishbel's place now." She pointed out of the window. "See there! Those are your brothers and sisters running home from school. We'd better get the scones buttered and then we'll get all the chores done so that everything is spick and span for Daddy coming home tomorrow."

As soon as Angus was set down on the floor he propelled himself towards the door, waiting eagerly to welcome his siblings back – especially his sister, Katie, who had taken over as his second mother since August when Morag had left to attend a secondary school in Edinburgh. Morag – who'd been such a help indoors and out – was sorely missed, especially by Hannah. There was no one who could keep the family supplied with water the way she could. Small in stature though she was, it seemed no problem for her to carry two brimming pailfuls of water up the hill with a wooden yoke about her neck. She could milk a cow, herd the sheep and tend the horses, though wise enough to leave collecting the hens' eggs to (as she saw it) her less capable brothers.

Allowing Morag to attend a grammar school on the mainland hadn't been a tough decision for Hannah and Jamie. She'd had an excellent primary education at the small school on Herrig – a better education, they felt, than she could have gained on the mainland. Classes were small and individual attention was something to be taken for granted rather than wished for. Having a very close relationship with Rachel, Morag had chosen to stay with her grandmother in Edinburgh and was now enrolled as a pupil at St Thomas Aquinas, a girls-only school. Her acceptance there had delighted Rachel, who pointed out that Morag having passed the qualifying examination with flying colours only confirmed what she'd always known – that she took her natural intelligence from her mother's side of the family. Rachel, of course, ignored the fact that Morag's father had been one of the youngest ever to pass his seagoing Master's ticket!

Angus looked up expectantly when he heard both the outside and inside doors bang open noisily; but it was Fergus, not Kate, who burst into the living room. Fergus was a sensitive lad who believed that whenever his father was away fishing he himself was responsible for the whole family. "Mathair," he excitedly cried and went on to babble a long spiel in Gaelic.

"Fergus! Oh, Fergus!" pleaded Hannah as she tried to calm him. "You know I haven't the Gaelic, so please talk to me in English."

Fergus hung his head apologetically. He always forgot that his mother was the only person on Herrig not to have the Gaelic. To be truthful, Gaelic was his first language, the language he loved best. It had been as a toddler, while sitting on the knees of his two great aunts, Ishbel and Myrtle, that he'd been taught to speak and sing in the ancient tongue. How grateful he felt towards them both for teaching him so effortlessly: no wonder that when they'd died five years ago, within weeks of one another, he had been quite distraught. Nevertheless, he continued to perfect his knowledge of the language by conversing at great length with his father and with all the others who chose to use the foreign English tongue only when the uneducated were about! With a patient sigh he announced, "Mum, the headmaster's just told us the fishing forecast is warning that there's a big storm brewing and our boats will be heading for shelter."

Hannah grimaced. "Och, is that not just like the thing. Here am I needing your father home tomorrow and now . . . Did the forecast say how long it would last?"

Making for the door, Fergus shook his head. "No. So I'll away and see to the beasts and hens and then do the locking up."

"Aye, you do that." Then, wagging a finger at Roddy, her second son, she firmly ordered him, "And once you've finished jamming that piece for yourself, Roddy, just you get outside and give Fergus a hand." Ever since he was just a toddler, Hannah had acknowledged that Roddy was exactly like her own brother Paul – always first to be at the table when a meal was being dished up but all too quick to disappear whenever there was work to be done. Until now she'd managed to make sure he didn't avoid his share of the chores but as he grew older it was increasingly hard to keep tabs on him. As Roddy made for the door, she focused her attention on Katie. "And you, my lass, could you go now and fill the pails with water? And this time try to have a few drops left in the bucket when you get back to the house!"

The storm raged throughout the night but had blown itself out by mid-morning and the sea was now perfectly calm – so calm that it resembled a sheet of glass. Hannah always said a silent prayer after such a storm was over. She was thankful that the damage this time was no more than a few slates off the roof.

It was mid-afternoon, while she was breastfeeding Ishbel, with Angus lying beside her on the couch having his afternoon nap, that she heard a soft tap on the outside door and then the door slowly creaking open. Quickly, she snatched her breast from Ishbel's mouth, causing the baby to cry out in some distress. But when Hannah saw that her visitor was Father Donald she was thankful she'd fastened up her blouse and made herself respectable. "Nice of you to call, Father," said Hannah with a beaming smile that died on her face once she saw that he had come with Peggy Mack in tow.

Peggy Mack had been a good friend to Hannah – the best friend she had on the island since Myrtle and Ishbel had died. Sure, it was Peggy Mack who'd shown her how to cut peat, plant potatoes in the lazybeds and herd the ponies. And it was Peggy Mack who would always hold the fort until Rachel arrived whenever another of her children was on the way. Most important of all, it was Peggy Mack who had schooled her in the ways of the island and who insisted that people speak English and not the Gaelic when she was about. But Hannah's first thought was of Peggy's brother, Calum, who had the second sight – and immediately a sickening feeling of dread filled Hannah's breast. "And what brings you here in the middle of the day, Peggy? Not got enough to do?" she asked shakily, trying hard to calm herself.

Father Donald stood back to let Peggy Mack sit on the settee beside Hannah. "Hannah, my dear . . ." he began tentatively.

"There's been an accident on the fishing boat," Peggy broke in, grasping Hannah's hand.

"Oh, no!" Hannah blurted out, pulling her hand free. "Please don't say something has happened to my own Jamie?"

Father Donald shook his head. "We're not quite sure yet. You see, as you know, I have the only telephone on the island. However, there are times, like today, when it doesn't work all that well." He hesitated. "But a garbled message did get through from Father Archie in Mallaig . . . I'm just not a hundred per cent positive, that when he said 'Jamie McKinley', whether he meant *your* Jamie the Bull or his cousin, Jamie McKinley the Fish. And before I could ask for clarification we were cut off. So all I am sure of is that an accident happened to a Jamie McKinley who was sailing on the Santa Maria."

Hannah looked perplexed. "An accident? So whoever it is will be in the hospital?"

Peggy and Father Donald shook their heads in unison.

"You mean the accident was . . ." Hannah just couldn't bring herself to say the word 'fatal'. All she could think of was the day she'd first stepped foot on the Isle of Herrig. Three old islanders were seated down on the pier, passing the time of day. Having alighted from the ferry-boat, she'd taken her head-square off and allowed her long blonde hair, with its ginger highlights, to tumble free in the fresh air. One of the old men, Peggy's brother Calum, on seeing her hair, had half-risen and gasped in horror before pointing a gnarled finger towards her. "It's her! It's her!" he'd shouted and gesturing to Hannah to get back on board the boat. "It's she that I've seen weeping on the shore. Go! Go home, lassie, while you have the chance."

Jamie had immediately gone over to Calum and grabbed him by the arm. Hannah had no idea what he'd said since the talk was all in Gaelic. Some months later, however, one of the busybodies of the island told her that for twenty years and more Calum had frequently foretold of a stranger, with long, flowing blonde hair, who would marry one of the islanders and make her home here. One day, so Calum had predicted, that woman would know great sorrow – a sorrow that had to do with her standing upon the shore, surrounded by many, many children. They would all be weeping as a fishing boat with a coffin on board would pass by on its way to tie up at the pier.

"Fatal, yes," mumbled Peggy, "but it shouldn't have been. He only banged his head when he slipped *jumping* from the boat onto the pier," she continued vehemently before whispering, "although you'll remember, Hannah, my dear, how our Calum *did* . . ."

Hannah shook her head violently. She just couldn't understand it. It was quite true that, since she'd made her home on the island, Calum had accurately foretold of two unnatural passings! But here they were, saying they weren't sure – and in any case why should anyone believe the ravings of an old man? "When will we know for sure?" she asked.

Father Donald put up his hand to silence Peggy before she could speak. "Well," he began, "as Jamie the Fish is the cousin of Father Archie at Mallaig, I would have expected him to ask me to call on his aunt immediately – the boy's mother. But, when he rang me . . ."

Father Donald didn't need to finish. Hannah already knew for sure. She rose and handed baby Ishbel to Peggy before saying, "You'll have to excuse me but I must go to the call-box and get in touch with my people." Her voice was quivering when she said, "I need my mother here – I want my mother."

Peggy threw her arms round Hannah and whispered in her ear, "The Father here has been in touch with the priest at Marionville and he's going to get in touch right away with your brother Sam."

Sam was in the mess room having his break. He had just fried up a couple of herring that Pete had dipped in oatmeal for him when the desk clerk rang through to say there was a priest who wanted to speak with him. And no, nobody else would do. Before rising to go to the outer office, Sam threw Pete a warning glance. He thought this had better not be another complaint about Pete running a club for single mothers – at which he was the only male! Sam was relieved therefore when he learned it wasn't Father Paddy O'Malley of St Margaret Mary's but the friendly priest, Paddy O'Boyle from St Ninian's at Marionville, whom he'd known so well ever since his juvenile football days. Both of them remained keen to encourage the local lads in a healthy sport that kept them out of trouble. And he had been so support-ive of Morag ever since she'd come to stay at Learig Close.

Sam extended his hand to Paddy. "Nice to see you, Paddy. And what can I do for you?"

Paddy looked about. "Is there somewhere private where we could have a chat?"

Sam beckoned Paddy to follow him through to the Inspector's room. Fortunately the inspector was at Gayfield and the room was vacant.

"Sam," Paddy began in a sympathetic tone. Sam immediately thought he had come to tell him that Johnny, the father who had long since deserted the family, was either dead or dying.

"I guess it's not good news."

Paddy shook his head.

"My father, is it?"

Paddy looked at Sam in some puzzlement, wondering why Sam should expect him to come with news of his father. Obviously Sam would have had a father but in all the years he'd known Sam, he had never heard him speak of his father.

" 'Fraid not," Paddy eventually answered and then faced up to the hard task of giving the devastating news from Herrig.

Ten minutes after Paddy had left Sam was still sitting there, trying to take in what he'd been told. He knew he should already be on his way to tell his mother and book a flight to Benbecula; yet all he wanted to do was to scream. To accuse this God, that Hannah put so much faith in, of betraying his precious family yet again. Sam's thoughts flew back to their childhood days. Days that should always have been filled with sunshine and laughter but were all too often cursed with desertion, poverty and hardship. He remembered how, as just a stripling, he had been prepared to do anything to help ease the predicaments that they regularly found themselves in. A slight smile came to his face as he remembered how he and Carrie once had to rob Gabby, their drunken grandfather, so that they wouldn't be evicted for rent arrears. Surely, he thought, they'd known quite enough sorrow without it continuing. This was not at all what he wanted for

Hannah and her large but happy brood. Unfortunately, not even robbing a bank, as he'd threatened to do when they were children, could change things this time. Firmly suppressing these angry fantasies, Sam reached out for the telephone directory. They needed to get to Hannah as fast as possible – and at least he had the wherewithal nowadays to do that without being dependent on his native wit to find it.

Sam collected Carrie on his way up to Learig Close. "Oh, Sam," Carrie pleaded, "tell me this is just a nightmare, that it's not true and I'm only dreaming!"

Sam said nothing. Deep in thought, he wondered if Hannah would be like Rachel and manage against all the odds to bring up her children unaided. But in Hannah's case it wasn't just the children – there were the thirty sheep and twenty hens, a cow and three ponies all needing looked after with equal care. And would she stay on an island where she was the only one who didn't have the Gaelic? Well, Sam conceded, he could be of some help. After all, here he was at the age of thirty and still unmarried. The only two females in his life who depended on him both had four paws and shaggy coats.

"It seems such a pity that there were only two seats left on the plane tomorrow," Carrie remarked, breaking into Sam's thoughts.

"Aye, it would have made such a difference to everybody if you and I could have gone too. But that's life, damn it!"

There had been no problem for Sam to take the time off to see Rachel and Morag safely on the plane at Glasgow. One of the things that the police were good at was looking after their own. All the same, as they neared the airport terminal Sam grew apprehensive. Rachel and Morag had never flown before. To be truthful, the only two in the family to have done so were Alice, when she flew out to live in Canada, and Paul – who had honeymooned with Yvonne on the Costa Brava no less. But his mother Rachel had never travelled further than Carlisle to see Jeannie, Auntie Bella's daughter, and when she visited Hannah it was always by the ferry. So how would she cope today, especially on a journey she'd hoped never to be making? And there was Morag too, who was trying so hard to be brave but whose heart was bursting at the thought of never seeing her beloved Daddy again.

Sam waited until the flight had taken off before he reluctantly made to leave the airport. At the check-in desk he had asked if there were any cancellations as he'd have then jumped aboard with his Mum and Morag – but no luck. All he could do was to cradle Morag in his arms and whisper in her ear to tell her Mum that he'd be up as soon as ever he could. And he'd take on the responsibility of building the extension that would house a bathroom when the water was linked up in late summer. Then he faced Rachel: but both mother and son realised they were too full of rage and grief to speak. Silence was the only option.

The day after Jamie's funeral, Rachel and Hannah went out for a walk together. Before they knew it, they were at the cemetery gate and Hannah was half-running towards Jamie's grave. Kneeling on the damp earth, she began to pat the mound below which her husband lay. "We'll need to get him a nice headstone," she said, looking up at her mother.

"True," agreed Rachel, thinking this was likely the best time to talk to Hannah – time when they wouldn't be disturbed by children or well-meaning neighbours. "But there are other things we have to sort out first."

"Like the children and me coming home to live with you?"

Shaking her head, Rachel instantly answered, "Home, Hannah? *This is* your home. Your children have known nowhere else but this island where they can roam free. Can you imagine even trying to get them all to stay on the pavement and keep a lookout for traffic? Not to mention the fact that this is where Jamie would want them to bide."

Tears welled up in Hannah's eyes as she broke in: "It's just that I thought I'd manage a lot better if I had you to help me. You coped so well when you were left to fend for us without a man's help."

Instead of offering Hannah a handkerchief, Rachel leant over and gently patted Hannah's face dry. "There!" she said, as if Hannah were a child once more. "You'll just have to be brave. The children didn't ask to be born and now it's your duty to do your very best for them. And what they certainly don't need, Hannah, is a mother who is always crying. Remember, they're hurting too and they're bearing up for you."

The effect of Rachel's lecture had Hannah burst into uncontrollable sobbing which Rachel made no attempt to control. Instead, she earnestly counselled her daughter to get it all out. Eventually, through complete exhaustion, Hannah stopped crying and, seizing the handkerchief from her mother, wiped away the last of her tears. "And is there any other advice you would like to give me?" she asked bitterly.

"Well, I know you have never liked talking about it, but with Jamie being . . ." Rachel hesitated as she detested using the word illegitimate, having only escaped being branded that herself because her drunken father, in the Leith Poorhouse, had succumbed to pressure and married her dying mother – her dear mother whose last wish was to lift the stigma of illegitimacy from her three-month-old baby, so she quietly continued ". . . being born out of wedlock – are you sure you'll get possession of the croft?"

Hannah looked up slowly but was unable to hide the look of bewilderment that rushed to her face. Of course, she told herself, Rachel was remembering how, after the death of Ishbel and Myrtle, Jamie's two old aunts who had brought him up, hadn't there been a worry that as Jamie, who was illegitimate and therefore had no rights of succession, would be ousted should a legal relative lay claim to the croft land and house? In the past Jamie had just bowed his head and accepted all the abuse and injustices that his bastard status provoked and had it come to that he would have accepted the loss of the croft as another unfair inevitability. However, ever since Hannah became his wife, he had never again apologised for something that wasn't his fault – oh yes, it was Hannah who had given him the courage to believe in himself and had imbued him with reasons to hold his head up high. And so, when the time came, he did not hesitate – as the adopted son, a son his two dear aunts had reared as their own, a son they were so proud of, a son who had made their life worth living – to petition the Crofters' Commission who without question had immediately awarded him what was morally his!

"Yes, Mum, the croft is ours." Hannah, who had never discussed Jamie's submission to the Crofters' Commission with anyone, added thoughtfully, "Well, not exactly mine . . ."

"What do you mean – not exactly yours?"

"Just that under croft law the eldest son inherits and that's Fergus."

Rachel relaxed. "So you're safe for now?"

"Not just for now, Mum. My Fergus will always see to it that I have a home."

"Good! So that just leaves two things to get settled."

"And what are those?"

"Firstly, I'll come here to Herrig as often as I can. And so will Sam and Carrie."

"And Paul?"

"Well, since he married Yvonne and bought a bungalow in Sydney Terrace he hasn't got much time for family."

"You don't get on too well with Yvonne, do you?"

"When dirt rises it blinds you," was all Rachel replied, which told Hannah everything about Rachel and Yvonne's relationship. "But, as I was saying, I'll come as often as I can and I'll find another job to help you out financially. Send parcels every week, I will."

Hannah smiled. This was the old Rachel – shoulders to the wheel and courage screwed to the sticking place. "And the other thing?"

"Morag. I'll leave her here for now. It'll soon be Christmas. But as soon as January comes she must come back to have her education in Edinburgh."

"Well, I thought she might like to be with us . . ."

"She's bright, Hannah, very bright, so she must get her chances. Unlike when you were young, there are plenty of us about to help you see that she does."

12
BROTHERLY LOVE

As Sam and Pimpernel Pete approached Silverknowes Parkway South, Sam still felt that the Deputy Chief Constable was ignoring the fact that the Drylaw Station from which they operated was the busiest not only in Edinburgh but also – if recent reports were to be believed – in the whole of Europe. In Sam's eyes it was therefore all the more unreasonable, if not bizarre, that the DCC should decide to send the pair of them to interview and placate a certain Mr Wilfred Boland who apparently wished to register a complaint.

Arriving at the front door, Pete pressed the bell with a flourish. As time ticked by with no obvious response from the resident, Sam had ample time to inspect Mr Boland's garden. A square, meticulously-manicured lawn was bordered by four rectangular flower beds, each filled with blooms of an identical height and species, all standing rigidly to attention. The scene made him wonder why some people liked such uniformity in a garden where, in his opinion, nature should be allowed to blossom freely. His gaze took in the straight paved pathway where not a single weed had been allowed to emerge from the smallest crevice. Shaking his head and smiling to himself, Sam imagined how the owner of the garden would react to a dog of independent mind wishing to do its business there.

With growing impatience, Pete rang the bell again and simultaneously hammered on the door. Almost at once the door was opened wide. "Oh, so I see you don't like to be kept waiting?" sneered the figure they presumed to be

Mr Wilfred Boland. This remark led both men to conclude that Mr Boland had been standing behind the door ever since their arrival.

"Our Deputy Chief Constable has asked us to come over and interview you with the aim of trying to find a solution to your problem," stated Sam politely, as Mr Boland edged aside just far enough to allow Sam and Pete a distinctly reluctant entry to his private domain.

After closing the outside door, double-locking it carefully and then pocketing the key, Mr Boland led the two officers into the lounge. Once there and having declined to offer them the convenience of a seat, he immediately launched into his tirade. "Every day now for a whole year," he emphasised by wagging his finger at Sam, "I have complained to you officers about a dog, a very large and excessively well-fed dog, fouling the entrance to my pathway."

"That's perfectly correct," replied Sam, "and our beat men, one of whom is Constable Capaldi here, have regularly inspected your property on their rounds and have never managed to catch sight of the offending animal."

Pointing to Pete, Mr Boland retaliated: "And I've never seen *that* beat man giving any attention whatsoever to my pathway at two and three in the morning when the culprit strikes. But perhaps that will be because he's too busy inspecting elsewhere!"

Sam looked directly at Pete, hoping for an explanation of some kind and wondering if the rumours he had heard about Pete keeping a pert little blonde happy while her husband was on nightshift had any credibility. And when Pete just beamed him the most engaging of smiles before placing himself behind Mr Boland, Sam knew for certain that the rumours were true!

Mr Boland then strode to the window and indicated that Sam and Pete should follow him. Once assured of their full attention, he pointed to the exact spot where the daily deposit was made. "Oh yes," Mr Boland continued, quite unaware that Sam was only half-listening. "I sit at my bedroom window all night long and at the exact moment when I have to interrupt my vigil in order to relieve myself – it's then that the beast strikes! And when I return to my post, all I can see is the beast's steaming calling-card." Drumming his fingers on the window pane, Mr Boland gave a deep sigh before going on. "As I have said to your Deputy, it's as if the animal had a spy who tells him whenever I'm off watch for an instant."

The mention of the Deputy made Sam turn from the window to give his complete attention to Mr Boland. "Yes. Now please tell me, Mr Boland, how was it you were able to get directly through to the Deputy?"

"Oh, I've tried to do so on many, many occasions without success. I knew therefore that I had to take drastic action to get him to listen."

"Such as?"

"By telling the telephone operator that the police force was blatantly and irresponsibly ignoring the fact that an alien plot to pollute the whole of Edinburgh with dog excrement was imminent – the danger being now at Level Five, one might say."

That remark was enough to make Sam realise there would be no placating Mr Boland and that diplomacy of the highest order was called for. "Well, Mr Boland," he began, "please accept that I fully appreciate how annoying this problem must be to you; but short of stationing a police officer at your gate for twenty-four hours every day, which we do not have the staffing levels to accommodate, I cannot really see what else we can do."

Mr Boland sank down in a chair and shook his head in bewilderment. "You, a police sergeant who, so I believe, is at this present time an Acting Inspector?" he spluttered. "You don't know what to do? No wonder you're just – *acting*."

Sam didn't react to the slight, being much too busy trying to stop himself from laughing at Pete who was making outrageous gestures behind Mr Boland's back. The pause allowed Mr Boland to continue, "You don't know what to do? Well, let me inform you what you *should* do. Round up every dog in this district. Take them all to the police compound, feed them, and then wait for them to relieve themselves so that you may . . ." Mr Boland went back to the windowsill where he picked up a jam jar, plainly containing a liberal quantity of canine excreta, and handed the container to Sam, ". . . compare it with this morning's sample!"

Sam accepted the evidence with some reluctance and indicated to Pete that it was time to leave. With considerable relief the two officers made their escape into the mad, mad outdoor world, neither saying anything until they were safely seated once more in the divisional car. Handing the jam jar to Pete, Sam asked, "What d'ye make of all that then?"

To which Pete replied with a wink and a chuckle, "Personally, I think it's all just a load of shit."

"Precisely!" agreed his friend.

From the mess hall telephone, Sam was completing his report to the Deputy about his meeting with Mr Boland, feeling rather gratified with himself that he had done so without allowing a hint of criticism into his voice. He concluded by calmly stating that in his opinion Mr Boland was at least extremely eccentric if not in need of some serious counselling. The Deputy, having listened to Sam's unbiased assessment of the situation, could only agree with Sam's findings and promised to write personally to Mr Boland. He would patiently explain that in years to come the police force might well possess the requisite technology and the manpower resources to test all canine stools within a square mile and thus identify the culprit but at this moment in time such expertise was not available to them.

Just as Sam was thanking the Deputy, the mess room door flew open and the station clerk announced loudly that Sam was needed in the station office as there was a serious and potentially fatal incident down at Inverleith. The Deputy, all too conscious of his force's priorities, advised Sam to forget all about Mr Boland and turn his full attention to more serious matters. Replacing the phone, Sam muttered to himself, "Devote myself to more serious matters? Great! In that case I'll never need to speak to Mr Wilfred Boland again!"

Immediately, Sam motioned the clerk to come further into the room and give his report. At the same time he asked his shift sergeant, Graham McNiven, to join him and listen to the story being imparted. It transpired that the clerk had taken a frantic call from the house-owner at 4 Botanic Mews, reporting that it seemed more than probable that murder most foul had been committed at number two, the house adjoining her own. She had reached that conclusion on the basis of all the shouting and screaming coming from the house in the early hours of that morning. Moreover, the neighbour's cats had not been let out as usual and had missed their customary morning treat provided by the caller.

Sam watched the expressions on Graham's face change from the affable to the incredulous. Thanking the clerk, Sam gestured to Graham and tersely said, "Let's get going."

"Right, sir," said Graham, putting on his cap at once. "Wonder what exactly the problem is down at Botanic Mews."

Sam shrugged his shoulders. "Now, Graham, before we go – where exactly is Botanic Mews?"

"You know, sir, surely. Just behind the Royal Botanic Gardens."

"Of course. I should have known." Sam's thoughts were focused on the caller's concern about the cats and he declared, "Know something? I'm right off animals the day. Never mind. Come on, Graham, and you too, son," he added, turning to the constable, Harry Troupe, who was happily demolishing a bacon roll.

Once back in the police car they sped towards Botanic Mews – a small but decidedly up-market *cul de sac*. With its blue lights flashing, their vehicle screeched to a halt and Sam couldn't help but notice how tranquil and beautiful the house and gardens of number two appeared. And yet there was something quite disturbing about the square and immaculate lawn, which painfully resembled Mr Boland's in that it seemed to have been manicured by hand rather than having been mown. The flower beds too were virtually identical to those in Wilfred Boland's beds, being set in regimented squares with their flowers all of an equal height and organised in strict colour rotation.

Glancing at the windows, Sam noticed that the curtains and blinds were all hung uniformly. Before he could speculate further about the motives of the people who felt compelled to dwell in the midst of such obsessive rigidity, the next-door neighbour appeared at his side.

"I always knew it would come to this!" the woman announced emphatically.

"And you are . . . ?" Sam asked.

"Mrs Doreen Smythe. I reside at number four."

Sam methodically extracted his notebook and began to write down these details.

"He's been pretending these last few weeks that he was still in employment, but I know that the printing firm he worked for has gone into administration." Writing busily, Sam made no comment and allowed the woman to ramble on. "My son, who is a reporter for a London-based news-paper, informed me of the fact eight weeks ago."

Sam felt inclined to tell Mrs Smythe he was surprised that her son only worked for a newspaper because if he was anything like his mother he ought to be publishing his own. Restraining himself, he simply asked if there was a pathway around the house that might allow him entry.

"No!" came the sharp retort. "Keeps his place locked up more securely than Fort Knox."

"Any chance of gaining entry through *your* back garden, Mrs Smythe?"

The woman hesitated. "Well, I suppose, in the interests of the cats' welfare, I might permit you access to my property. But only yourself, Inspector, you understand. I do *not* wish junior ranks with muddy feet trailing over my Wilton!"

Ignoring Mrs Smythe's conditions, Sam beckoned Graham and Harry to follow him as he made an elaborate display of wiping his feet spotlessly clean on the doormat.

Once all three had emerged from the back door and clambered over the wall into the back garden of number two, it immediately became obvious they could only enter the house by breaking a side window. And once that was done, it was Sam of course, being the thinnest and fittest, who alone could squeeze through, hampered severely by a flurry of fur and the patter of paws as the three imprisoned cats desperately made good their escape over his body. With some relief he landed head first on the floor and instantly became aware of a cloying smell that reminded him vividly of Leith Hospital. The stench, he reckoned, was emanating from behind the kitchen door, but before proceeding any further he unlocked the back door and admitted his two colleagues. "Graham, you stay right here and don't allow *anyone* past that door. Especially the lady from number four!" Sam emphasised as he pointed to the back door. "And you, Harry, come with me so that I've got a witness while I search this house."

The two men immediately headed for what proved to be the lounge. Here, the smell – which Sam by now had identified as ether – was quite overpowering. With the aim of opening a window Sam took a few steps forward, only to find his feet obstructed by two bodies lying behind the settee. One proved to be that of a rather pretty woman in early middle age, lying wide-eyed but unseeing, having obviously been subdued by the ether before being stabbed in the throat. The other was a man of similar age whose wrists had been cut and who was lying across the female body. A large carving knife lay close by. At once Sam turned to Harry, who by now was retching uncontrollably.

"This your first time at a . . ." Sam hesitated before adding, ". . . at a violent death?" Harry nodded but words were beyond him. "Right then, my lad. You skedaddle back to Graham and tell him to phone CID and have them get down here pronto. Then take a dander around the gardens."

Harry looked puzzled.

"Ye ken what I mean," Sam explained patiently. "The Botanics of course! Get yourself some good fresh air there. Now off with you while I seal off this crime scene."

It was when he went over to the bodies once more to make certain there was no sign of life that the male figure uttered a faint moan. Sam shouted after Harry to tell Graham to call an ambulance. Bending down in an effort to clear the man's airways, he wondered what could make a man murder his wife. In fact, he wondered why any human being would want to end the life of another. Sam's thoughts flew back to his own childhood and to his feelings of terror when his mother and father were having yet another of their frequent heated arguments. He instantly recalled the time when his mother had lifted a hatchet menacingly with every indication of being about to smash it into his father's skull. He could still picture only too clearly the colour draining from his father's face as his knees buckled. Deadly white his father had lain there – just as bloodless as that poor lassie lying dead on the floor in front of him. It was Sam's big sister, Hannah, who had managed to wrest the hatchet from his mother's grasp, had chucked it into the glory-hole and had quickly closed the hatch door on it. Sam could still hear the heavy metallic clang that it made when it hit the stone floor. After that, the only sound was that of his mother bitterly hissing into his father's ear: "You're not even worth swinging for!" Those memories also triggered a mental reminder that he'd been told just the other day that his father, Johnny, was now very ill and in the City Hospital. Perhaps he should speak to Carrie about going to visit him there. On second thought, he wondered if he should even bother. After all, Johnny had never sought *him* out in all those years since his departure from the family home.

When the CID arrived, Sam was somewhat surprised to find that newly promoted Superintendent Paul Campbell was in charge. With an outstretched hand and proud smile lighting up his face, Sam approached his brother. Ignoring the gesture, Paul ordered that all personnel other than his own CID squad should leave the house and wait in the garden.

"But, Paul," Sam interrupted, "I was the first officer on the scene and I need to give you my report."

Paul made no answer other than to indicate with an abrupt jerk of his thumb that Sam should join the other uniformed officers in the back garden.

Humiliated, Sam strode purposefully out of the house and summoned Graham and Harry to join him in the divisional car. With the three on board Sam then drove the vehicle at a leisurely pace out of Botanic Mews. No one spoke.

By the time they had returned to Drylaw Substation the duty clerk was out in the driveway and signalling urgently to Sam to wind down his window. Sam did so and asked, "A problem, is there?"

"Y-yes," stammered the clerk, "you've to return immediately to the scene of the crime at Botanic Mews. The Super also wants to know why you left without seeking his permission."

Sam wound up the window and put the car into gear but, instead of heading back down the road as instructed, he steered their car over to the parking bay and switched off the engine. Jumping from the vehicle, he made his way into the office. "Summations!" he demanded of the clerk. Quickly, the clerk handed over his list of all the occurrences since the shift had begun and Sam meticulously checked each incident, asking in-depth questions about each event. Once he had initialled each item and satisfied himself that the subdivision was running as he wished, he sat down next to the clerk whom he instructed to type out a statement detailing precisely the police involvement in Botanic Mews from the moment of his arrival at the scene of crime until Paul's appearance. Once satisfied with the statement, he took it from the clerk, signed it and safely lodged it in his breast pocket. Then, instead of complying with yet a further request from Paul to return to the crime locus, he strolled along to the mess room and made himself a cup of instant coffee. He had just added the milk to the cup and raised it to his mouth when the duty clerk, who couldn't fail to hide his embarrassment, came into the room to inform him that the Superintendent was now blowing a gasket – and demanding that Sam return to Botanic Mews without a moment's delay. The clerk was now pleading to Sam with his eyes. "What will I say to the Super now?"

Sam chuckled before answering. "Just tell him what I told you to say the last time – that I'll comply with his request just as soon as my duties permit." However, a further fifteen minutes were to elapse before he would condescend to adhere to his brother's request.

More than an hour had passed since Sam had left Botanic Mews before Graham eventually chauffeured him back to the crime scene. He had stepped leisurely out of the vehicle when Paul leapt towards him.

"What the hell d'ye think you're playing at?"

Sam smiled and nonchalantly indicated to Paul that they should move indoors and have their conversation there.

"I repeat," Paul snarled, once they were installed in the dining room that had obviously been taken over as the command centre. "What *do* you think you're up to, leaving the scene like that?"

Sam sat down at the table, facing his brother. "You made a complete fool of me and my men. We were made to feel, as the CID always wants, just like uniformed numpties."

"I was only trying to take charge and stop any further contamination of the crime scene by your clumsy . . ." Paul stopped in embarrassment before going on, "I mean your untrained officers."

"No you weren't, sonny boy. You were trying to be seen as the big man. Well, let me tell you, and tell you good: you do *not* dismiss me, or anyone else, with the contempt you showed when you arrived here this morning. And a man in your position should be doing all he can to end the tension that exists between CID and the uniformed branches – not make it worse!"

Paul bristled. He didn't like being reminded of his obligations. "I know what's wrong with you," he retorted, "you're simply jealous because I'm getting on better than you."

Sam laughed aloud. "Look, I could have gone to the CID but it wasn't for me. I like being a community guy. I don't want to be up to my knees in blood and tears every weekend."

"Says you. But, as Yvonne says, I'm a cut above anybody else in the family."

"So that's what it's all about, is it? Mrs Hoity-toity, the royal fishwife, getting above herself?"

"No she isn't. She's an asset to me. And if you'd asked for her help when Hannah's Jamie was killed, you'd have got it. But we weren't even told – never mind not being asked to the funeral."

"Only Mam was at the funeral. And just ask yourself this, Paul. When have you ever done anything for the family since you and darling Yvonne got hitched?"

"Yvonne has a position to keep up. She's an infant mistress now and how do you think it feels for her having to introduce people to Mam who's only a tea-lady at the hospital and who works in Kemp's bakery on the ovens."

Sam jumped from his chair and made a lunge at Paul as he yelled: "Believe me, sonny, *my* mother is a lady – a lady whose shoes your wife isn't good enough to clean – never mind fill." But instead of carrying out his threat to assault Paul, Sam took the report from his breast pocket and flung it towards him. "All you need to know about what happened in this house before your arrival is accurately detailed here. All that is, except for the reason for the needless tragedy that occurred here today. Which, in my opinion, was caused by someone being a social climber and forgetting his humble roots!"

13
BREAKERS AHEAD

Carrie had just gone into her office when she found Mrs Brockie, one of the school's dining attendants, waiting impatiently for her. "I'm so sorry," she said, taking off her coat and hanging it up.

"Aye, and so you should be. It's now gone half past eleven," pronounced Mrs Brockie with arms akimbo and her right foot tapping the floor irritably, "and you still haven't told us exactly how many will be for dinner the day."

"I really am sorry," Carrie replied as she sat down at her desk and began totalling up the figures, "but David Foster was hurt in the playground."

"Yon wee haemophilic laddie?"

"Aye. So Mr Hamilton phoned for a taxi and put David and me in it, telling the driver to get us to Leith hospital as quick as possible."

"Did you leave the wee lad there?"

"Not till Mr Hamilton arrived with David's mother. Then he drove me back up the road."

"A real guid man, that new headmaster of ours. Took on that haemophilic laddie without a second thought."

Refusing to be drawn into the controversy about David's admission to mainstream classes at Hermitage Park, Carrie merely remarked, "Well, he's certainly a change from his predecessor," who hadn't even looked like an educated man, let alone a headmaster. William Hamilton, on the other hand, was a man whom no child could fear because he looked so much like a benevolent grandfather, with his portly build, smiling face and somewhat amusing side-whiskers cultivated, Carrie was sure, to compensate for his balding crown. Like all men of his age, Willie Hamilton was not immune from personal vanity. But all she said to Mrs Brockie was, "And did you know he had once been a teacher here?"

"Away!"

"Aye, and a good one at that." Carrie face beamed with pride. "Taught my brother Paul, so he did. You know, the one that was promoted last week to Chief Superintendent."

"Your Paul promoted again?" Mrs Brockie said with a sniff before pursing her lips and chuckling, "And what about Sam? Is he still acting the goat?"

Carrie bristled. "Sam's turn will come, never you fear. And there's some that would say Sam's the better cop."

"No need to get shirty. I was just teasing. There's nobody a bigger fan of Sam than me. Oh aye, I'm that grateful, so very grateful, to him and yon Kennel Club he runs, for training my wee dog, Satan, to stop frae biting folk."

"Right enough. He did get your Alsatian to stop taking lumps out of folk. All, that is, bar the poor postie."

Mrs Brockie was about to retort that the postman, who never delivered anything to her but bills, could do with a good bite taken out of him, when the distinctive tap-tapping of the Infant Mistress's feet approaching the office made both women grimace. Quickly, Carrie stood up and thrust the dinner list into Mrs Brockie's hand, blurting out, "So sorry to have inconvenienced you, Mrs Brockie."

Delivering an obviously feigned cough, Miss King observed tartly, "Ahem! It's not only Mrs Brockie who is inconvenienced by her malingering and gossiping here, but my Infants who are going to have to wait for their midday meal."

Deciding, as everyone else did, that there was no point in arguing with Miss King, Mrs Brockie slipped smartly behind the headmaster's desk and fled out of the door.

Satisfied that Mrs Brockie had been effectively dealt with, Miss King turned to Carrie. "Now, Mrs Fraser. How did David fare at the hospital?"

Carrie smiled to herself. For all her frosty and standoffish manner, Miss King, like Mr Hamilton, truly cared about the welfare of all the children under her control. And, like the headmaster, she tried to enhance their lives by introducing them to the arts. Carrie remembered how two weeks ago most of the teaching staff had sniggered when Miss King had the children walk into school while Strauss's *Tales from the Vienna Woods* was being played in the background. The general opinion that day amongst the staff was that the children would have reacted better to Tony Bennett singing *Let's Call It a Day*. However, they were nonplussed later that week when the music teacher asked the children what music they preferred listening to and there was a resounding chorus of "Strauss!"

"Mrs Fraser, did you hear me? I asked you how David . . .?"

"There didn't seem to be a problem," Carrie hastily replied.

"Mrs Fraser, David suffers from haemophilia and a mere scratch could prove fatal."

Carrie blushed. "Yes, I know. What I meant was the hospital took over and his mother arrived so Mr Hamilton and I came back here."

Miss King nodded. "Now, whenever Mr Hamilton has the time, I *must* speak with him."

Carrie smiled and pointed to the door where Mr Hamilton was already standing.

"Ah, headmaster," began Miss King, "I was wondering if you would kindly have a word with Robert . . ." Miss King hesitated, "I mean Bobby Smith's father." She tut-tutted before adding, "Why parents should give their children truly noble names like Robert and then shorten them to Bobby I really don't know."

"Quite so," said Mr Hamilton amiably. "Now, if Robert, or Bobby, or whatever his name is, should be absent again then just have the attendance officer deal with it."

"I only wish I could. But poor Mr Good, who has been dealing with the Smith family for six months now, has gone off on long-term sick leave due to a nervous breakdown!"

Mr Hamilton was now seated in his chair. "So be it. Well, the next time Bobby attends school I'll make a point of speaking to his father." Mr Hamilton stroked his chin pensively, "Do I take it his father still escorts him to school?"

"Yes, along with the dog! And you won't need to wait to speak to him. He arrived with Bobby ten minutes ago."

Mr Hamilton sighed. "Just in time for Bobby to get his free lunch, I presume?"

"Precisely. But I told Mr Smith to wait in the corridor, since you would wish to see him."

Carrie could hear the barking of the Smiths' dog and, as it grew louder, she realised that Bobby's father was rapidly approaching the office. "Are you afraid of German Shepherds?" Mr Hamilton asked.

"Not at all," replied Carrie. "My brother has one and it's very well-behaved. But then my brother is one of the trainers at the Kennel Club."

Carrie had just finished speaking when an enormous brute of a dog, on a long leash, bounded into the office. Two more minutes elapsed, however, before a breathless and obese shambles of a man stumbled in, clutching the end of the dog's lead.

At the first sight of this awesome spectacle, Mr Hamilton's jaw dropped and he instinctively reached for the small hand bell used for summoning the janitor, Alex Logan. Within seconds, Alex's head appeared round the doorway but he seemed distinctly reluctant to take charge of the dog. "Look, sir," he complained, with no attempt to hide the incredulity in his voice, "it's on a blooming washing-line."

"Aye," interjected Mr Smith. "That's because my doctor says I've got a bad heart and as he's a big dog that needs a fair bit o exercise – well, yon lang rope means he can run all over the place while I just stand and let him gang about awyes."

By now the dog had circled Mr Hamilton's desk twice and there was still enough rope left for him to do another two laps. It took the janitor, assisted by Miss King, who ended up tied to the coat stand, a good five minutes to release Mr Hamilton, Miss King and the dog from the tangle. Once the janitor had unceremoniously dragged the reluctant dog from the office, Mr Smith thereupon demanded to know why Mr Hamilton wished to see him.

"We have to talk about Bobby's school attendance," began Mr Hamilton, then adding with a hint of gentle sarcasm, "or perhaps I should say his lack of attendance?"

"Aye, well," remarked Mr Smith complacently, "ye cannae really blame him. I mean, it's been a cold, cold, winter and even the noo – it's April, is it no? – it's still freezing."

The Headmaster gave a slight nod of assent. "That is so," he agreed, "but the other four hundred and ninety-nine children have all managed to attend." Mr Hamilton took a deep breath. "Look here, Mr Smith, I'm trying to help you and

Bobby. So is there anything you can think of that I could do that would solve the problem?"

Bobby's father offered no reply and only shifted his bulk uneasily in the chair. After a lengthy silence, Mr Hamilton continued, "Now, Mr Smith, the law says, as you're very well aware, that Bobby has to receive an education."

Mr Smith sat grim-faced and silent for several more minutes before his face muscles relaxed and he brightly announced, "I know! Maybe you could get him into my auld school. A great school that is. The bus takes you there and the bus brings you back hame."

Mr Hamilton was glad to be standing in front of his desk since it offered some much-needed support as his whole body sagged wearily against it. Dismayed and stunned, he asked, "Are you telling me you want to have Bobby transferred to Clarebank Special School?"

"Aye, I wouldnae be where I am the day if I hadn't gone there. D'ye ken this? They had me reading a book by the time I was ten years old!"

With all the delays of the day, it was a quarter to four before Carrie was ready to go home. She had just left the office when she became aware of a child sobbing. Listening intently, she deduced that the sound was emanating from the boys' cloakroom. On entering, she found an eight year old by the name of Jack Turnbull sitting on the floor in a flood of tears.

"Whatever's the matter?" asked Carrie, as she bent down to pull the child to his feet.

"It's ma coat. Somebody's nicked ma coat."

Carrie looked along the rails and saw that further away there was a black duffle coat hanging on a hook. "There," she said, pointing to the coat. "Isn't that your coat?"

Jack shook his head. By now Carrie had fetched the coat. "Look," she said, it's just right for your size."

Jack sniffed loudly. "Aye, but it's no mine!"

"How d'you know that?" asked Carrie who was now increasingly anxious to be home in time for her own children returning from school.

"Because it doesn't have gloves that flap like this!" And Jack now waved his hands up and down to demonstrate the point.

Carrie smiled. Jack's mother was not the brightest of persons and relied on her own mother to help her with Jack. Mrs Stoddart, Jack's Granny, who just adored her grandson, always made sure he was well-clad and – since Jack was like his mother in being a wee bit slow in the uptake and in keeping hold of his belongings – had devised all manner of simple techniques to keep him right. For instance, she still sewed his gloves on to a tape which she then threaded through the coat sleeves so that they couldn't get lost. "Right," agreed Carrie, "so this is not your coat. Someone must have taken yours by mistake and they'll bring it back tomorrow. You just put this one on then and get yourself off home before it gets any colder."

Jack shook his head. "You want me to get battered?" he snivelled.

"No. I just want you to get home safe and warm," Carrie coaxed as she held out the coat for Jack to put his arms through. "Good. Now, the Lollipop man will be away now, so I'll take you over to the other side of Lochend Road and you can run all the way home from there."

Carrie had given Sophie and Donald their evening meal, attended to their homework and settled them down to watch television by the time their father reached home. Will's face lit up at the sight of his children. He really was such a devoted father, working all the hours God sent to keep them as best he could. The moment Carrie had disappeared into the kitchen to heat up his supper, Will was down on the floor with Donald and had donned his son's tribal chief's feather headdress. The children were hysterical with laughter. They just loved it when their father played with them. Carrie thought she knew why they preferred his games to hers – it was because he was still a child at heart. And when Carrie, who was the one always to hand out the discipline, came back into the living room to announce that Will's meal was ready and remarked that, in her opinion, he didn't make a very convincing Cochise since he was going bald at the front of his head. Will's cheeky response of "Pale-face talk with forked tongue" was met with gales of laughter from the children.

But as the laughter subsided, Carrie noticed how tired Will was looking. Well, she reasoned to herself, he took on too much overtime. In addition to his straight shifts, he worked Tuesday and Thursday evenings, Saturday mornings and *all day* on Sundays because that was paid double-time.

Once the children were in bed and Will was watching *Double Your Money* on TV, Carrie grasped the opportunity to say, "Will, dearest, don't you think you're working too hard? What I mean is – now that the school roll is over five hundred and I've been allocated twenty-five hours' work, maybe you could give up your Sunday working."

Will made no answer and Carrie raised her voice: "Did you hear me, Will?"

"Aye, I did," came the eventual reply. "But I'm trying to save up for a wee car and I'd rather work Sundays to get it."

"A car!" exploded Carrie. "You said that renting the television from Radio Rentals would definitely be our last extravagance."

"And who was the first to break that promise?" retorted Will.

Carrie looked perplexed. "Surely you're not suggesting it was me."

"I am that. I mean, what d'you call that twin-tub washing machine in the kitchen then?"

"A necessity, of course," retorted Carrie. "Don't you realise *I* can't work at the school and still find time, like my mother, to go to the washhouse?"

"And life would be a lot easier for *me* if only I could drive myself back and forward to work."

Carrie had only just finished acquainting Miss King with the problem of Jack's coat when both boy and mother arrived at the office door. Instantly, Mrs Turnbull launched into a tirade – blaming the school for her son's missing coat that had the flapping gloves.

"Mrs Turnbull, I fully understand how annoying the loss of Jack's coat is to you," Miss King responded, with as much self-control as she could muster, "and once the school has assembled for the day you and I will search the cloakroom for it."

"You mean I've got to check through all the coats?"

"Yes, indeed. These days every child wears a black duffle coat, so that'll be five hundred we have to look through."

Once the children were all safely seated in their classes, Miss King, Mrs Turnbull and Carrie began a diligent search – which after some fifteen minutes proved fruitful. Miss King retrieved the coat and passed it to Mrs Turnbull, remarking gently, "You know, Mrs Turnbull, it would help greatly if Jack's name was on his coat."

Mrs Turnbull's eyes widened in disbelief as she stuttered, "Di-dinnae be daft. What use would that be? I mean it's thanks to you, being no good at your job, that my Jack cannae read!"

Carrie waited for some response from Miss King but none was forthcoming. She went back to her office thinking how she wished all her worries could be resolved as easily and quickly as the finding of Jack's coat. And, she admitted to herself, Will looking so tired was one of the main ones. Guilt began to take over as she acknowledged that next Friday, when the Easter holidays began, she would be off with the children to Herrig. It wasn't just that she wanted to see how Hannah was coping since Jamie's death; she also wanted to help. However, she wasn't sure that her mother's suggestion was a good idea. Rachel had said, "If you plant a good lot of potatoes now, there'll be enough when they get harvested in October to see Hannah through the winter." Sure enough, Will's father had taught her how to grow flowers from seed or cuttings, but did that qualify her for planting potatoes in lazybeds? She thought not!

Long after the ferry left the shore Carrie still remained standing at the rail, staring back towards the Oban dockside, even though Will and Sam had left the pier and made their way back to Sam's car. Such uncharacteristic inaction stemmed from her remaining doubts and indecision over Will's wellbeing. She had even persuaded Sam to coax Will into taking time off to play a couple of rounds of golf with him. Having just begun a sixteen-day holiday break, Sam had readily agreed: it would do him a world of good to have some relaxation before he and a squad of his tradesmen friends pitched up in Herrig next week. Sam had pondered long and hard on what he might do to make life easier for Hannah after Jamie's death. It was Rachel who'd put the idea into his head about building an extension that would house the bathroom. They would also finish putting in the drainage system which Jamie had begun. That would mean Hannah's croft house would be ready for the link-up when piped water became available in July.

Sophie and Donald, who had scampered off to explore the ferryboat, were now back at her side demanding to know when they could have a meal in the café.

"A meal in the café? You must be joking. You were fed on fish and chips in a restaurant just an hour ago," was their mother's impatient reply.

It took a full six hours for the journey from Oban to Barra and the children continued to pester their mother for a meal. Assuming that the next docking would be at Lochboisdale, only forty minutes away, Carrie at length judged it reasonable to allow the children to eat in the café – where everything came with chips – without the fear of Sophie being sick. As soon as the ferry set sail, a fresh breeze sprang up and quickly gathered momentum. By the time Sophie and Donald had finished their meal of pie, beans and chips, the wind was judged to be approaching gale force and the few passengers now remaining on board were urged to stay safely in the lounge area. Within another half hour the ferryboat was being tossed on the water like a cork and waves the height of houses were buffeting their vessel.

Carrie did her best to calm Sophie's fears as her face grew increasingly pale and she began to retch. Donald meanwhile kept running around the lounge, even venturing outside when his mother wasn't looking. When forcibly thrust back inside by one of the crew members he proudly proclaimed to all and sundry: "I've just seen Moby Dick!"

Carrie was about to order him to come and sit quietly beside her when Sophie, without any warning, vomited her whole meal – pie, beans and chips – straight into her mother's lap. Looking round for some help, Carrie became increasingly alarmed when she noticed that one of the remaining passengers, a nun who throughout the journey had sat in the corner, not engaging in conversation with anyone, now had her rosary beads out and was praying fervently. The only other person left was a youngish priest who immediately tried to come to Carrie's assistance. This proved difficult because of the boat's violent lurching and it took him some minutes to struggle over to her side. There he formally introduced himself as Father Charlie before he too threw up into Carrie's lap!

Completely undaunted by the storm, Donald had once again escaped outside and when he eventually returned his mother angrily grabbed him by the collar and yelled, "Look here, Donald, things are quite bad enough without you falling overboard. All I want right now is to get off this blinking boat!"

To which Donald solemnly commented: "You will – and right now, because it's sinking!"

An hour later, however, after three unsuccessful attempts to dock and repeatedly being blown off course, the ferryboat was finally moored safely at Lochboisdale. By that time Carrie had cleaned herself up passably and was anxious to get Sophie back on dry land, but because of all the delay and the wind's persisting fury she was firmly advised that there was no way anyone would ferry her over to Hannah's croft that night. All she could then do was hope to find bed and breakfast before reaching Herrig in the morning.

Standing disconsolately on the pier beside the children and her luggage, she was unexpectedly joined by Father Charlie who announced that he too was going to Herrig and that a fishing boat was already waiting for him. So why shouldn't they all go with him? Carrie looked down at the tiny craft bobbing wildly up and down in the water and politely declined the offer – that was, until two of the fishing boat's crew grabbed hold of her children and unhesitatingly jumped aboard with them. Carrie was still feeling terrified but the impossible idea of not being with her children on the perilous ten-minute journey made her throw caution to the winds; so when Father Charlie took her hand she closed her eyes and desperately leapt into space before landing unharmed on the rising boat deck.

The wind was still blowing so fiercely that the fishermen decided it would be wiser not to tie up at the pier on Herrig and to attempt a landing instead at a small, sheltered harbour on the leeward side of the island. This proved successful but once back on dry land Carrie grimaced, realising they'd have to scramble in the pitch dark all the way uphill before reaching the road that led to Hannah's croft. Once more the fishermen came to the rescue by proposing that, as the weather was so ferocious, everyone should pile on to the fish lorry. A few minutes later, Carrie, the children and Father Charlie were all safely and unceremoniously dumped at the foot of the slope that led up to Hannah's home.

On finally reaching the croft, however, Carrie was dismayed to find the house in total darkness. There was not a flicker of light or life. Impatiently, she repeatedly thumped on the door until finally the door opened and Hannah stood there, a coat flung hastily over her nightclothes and a glowing Tilley lamp in her hand. "Oh, it's you," she remarked, as if it was an everyday thing for a collection of soaking-wet, bedraggled people to arrive at one's door in the middle of the night. "Why are you knocking at the door?"

"Because we need to get inside and out of this drenching freezing cold, of course!" Carrie hissed between her clenched teeth.

Standing aside to let them come in, Hannah laughingly continued, "Then why didn't you just open the door and come in? It's never locked."

Once inside the house, Carrie's heart sank as she surveyed the disorder of the poorly-lit room. Washing waiting to be hung up outside was heaped upon a rickety wooden chair; children's shoes were scattered carelessly about the floor; the table was littered with dirty crockery; and the Raeburn cooker lay lifeless and cold, with pale grey ashes spilling from its metal ribs and dropping on to the hearth stone.

"I didn't expect you tonight," muttered Hannah, casually picking up some children's clothes from a chair so that Carrie might sit down. "What I mean is, you'd have to be plumb crazy to do the crossing on a night like this."

"The fishing boat waited for me so I offered your sister and her children a lift," Charlie explained quietly.

Only then did Hannah become aware of Father Charlie's presence and she now looked at him in some puzzlement.

"I'm Father Charlie from Glasgow," the priest explained. "I'm to be Father Donald's guest on Herrig for the next two weeks." Amazed by his youth and good looks, Hannah could only give a little bob of acknowledgement, but Carrie felt sure that if she hadn't been there her sister would have

172

curtseyed deeply to the priest. Instead, she held out her hand to him and announced primly that she was very pleased to meet him. Charlie responded by saying, "I must be going now. Is it just up the hill I have to go?" he asked, pointing vaguely upwards.

"No, wait," said Carrie. "At least let us offer you some supper in return for all you've done."

"Well, we could have if I hadn't already fed your supper to the children," Hannah said, pointing to the table that now only had a few crusts lying among the debris.

"You mean there's nothing for us to eat?"

"Well, there is, but it needs cooking."

"So where is it? I'll cook it," Carrie said firmly. Hannah shook her head.

"And why ever not? After all, you do have electricity now. And I know Mummy sent you up an electric cooker a couple of months back."

Hannah shook her head sadly. "Yes, that's all true – but the cooker doesn't work when the electricity is down."

Carrie now looked hopefully at the Raeburn.

"And that stove doesn't go if the wind is blowing from the north-west like it is tonight," added Hannah, who was beginning to feel Carrie was being really awkward now.

Before Carrie could say anything, she became aware that Sophie seemed to be in some kind of distress. It wasn't so much the laboured breathing that concerned her mother but the fact that she was performing a kind of war-dance that reverberated on the lino-covered floor.

"Sophie! Whatever in the name of goodness is wrong with you?"

"Oh Mummy," sobbed Sophie, "I need . . . I need to go to the bathroom and I need to go right now!"

"But we won't have a bathroom until next year," remarked Fergus, Hannah's eldest son, who had been wakened up by all the commotion.

"She just means she needs to use the lavatory," explained Carrie.

"Well, you're welcome to have the pail that we all use." Fergus opened the living room door and pointed to a decidedly grubby aluminium pail perched on the landing at the top of the stair.

Sophie's face contorted in alarm. "But what I have to do *can't* be done in a pail!"

"Don't tell me you have diarrhoea again." snapped Carrie impatiently.

Sophie took a deep breath and nodded her head furiously.

"So you'll just need to go to the cow byre," said Fergus calmly. "And you don't need to be frightened because I'll go with you," he added helpfully, liking the look of this new cousin and wanting to ingratiate himself.

By now, all of Hannah's children were awake and in the living room. Even Morag, who had come home from her Edinburgh school for the Easter holidays, had managed to haul herself out of bed. Quickly she intervened by saying, "Fergus, boys don't take girls to the cow byre. I'll do it," and, taking Sophie's hand, steered her towards the door. A moment later, Carrie found herself leaning forward in her chair to make room for three year old Myrtle who was trying to squeeze herself in behind her. Carrie smiled with pleasure and her grin turned to laughter when Myrtle flung both arms around Carrie's neck and whispered, "You are a *very* lucky woman, Auntie Carrie."

"Am I?" queried Carrie in some genuine surprise as she reached behind and took the child on to her knee.

"Yes, cos not only have you got the new blankets on your bed but Mummy also washed the sheets!"

Carrie felt the tears come to her eyes and knew she mustn't let them drop. That would have been just too cruel. But she was struggling with her emotions. She just couldn't stop thinking how easy life at home was for her. A twin-tub washing machine, sheets washed every week, a gas cooker that worked even when the electricity lines were blown down, a garden that could have won a prize – and all of those riches supplied by her Will who worked so hard to provide, just as Jamie had, for his family. She was still deep in such thoughts when Sophie rushed back into the room. This time she was doing an imitation of Waltzing Matilda and when Carrie demanded to know what the problem was now she spluttered, "Ooh, M-mummy, you said I'd have to use the cow byre but you n-never said the c-cow would still be in it!"

When Carrie looked towards Hannah for a solution, all her sister said was: "No, Carrie, we simply can't take the cow outside in such a gale. And even if I did, no doubt your Sophie would be wanting me to take out all the hens that are roosting up in the rafters there."

It was then that Father Charlie, who had been a silent spectator to all this drama, rose and gently suggested that, since Father Donald was the only one on the island who already had such modern facilities, might it not be a better idea if he took Sophie up there so that she could relieve herself in comfort. In fact he was sure that his colleague would also allow Carrie the comfort of Donald's one and only luxury!

Father Charlie was in no doubt as to what was in Carrie's mind. He knew she must be wondering why this priest, Father Donald, who lived all alone and had taken a vow of poverty, should have been the first to have a bathroom installed, complete with running water and flushing facilities, while there was Hannah and herself with eleven children between them and yet all the sanitation they had was a pail at the top of the stairs and a cow byre with the cow still inside it!

Sunbeams softly streaming through the bedroom window eventually wakened Carrie. When she'd at last gone to bed with Sophie and Donald she felt certain she'd never get to sleep. At home she was used to having a hot water bottle to take the chill off the sheets but here on Herrig there was no such luxury except perhaps for the very young. But now, she was thinking of snuggling down again when she heard movement from the living room and guessed that Hannah was already up and about.

Dressing herself quickly, she quietly made her way into the living room. Hannah, kneeling by the Raeburn and obviously struggling to set it going once more, was unaware of her presence and that offered Carrie the chance to study her sister. She judged that Hannah, whose shoulders now seemed permanently bowed and whose hair was now straggly and dull, in sharp contrast to its once tantalisingly lively and gleaming blonde, had reached that point in her bereavement when nature's anaesthetics have worn off and all that is left is the ice-cold reality of the loss. Carrie vividly recalled the vivacious girl Hannah had been and how fastidious she had been about both her appearance and her surroundings. Her thoughts turned to speculating about how things would work out for Hannah and all her children – when suddenly she became aware of movement in a pile of rags in the corner. "Hannah," she asked, pointing to the wriggling bundle, "what on earth is that?"

Her sister turned suddenly and seemed taken aback to see Carrie there. Then a smile came to her face and she explained, "Nothing for you to worry about, Carrie. It's just a lamb that was born two days ago. Its mother won't feed it so it has to be bottle-fed."

"Okay. But does it need to be in here?"

Hannah smiled again. "It will do no harm. No harm at all." She placed one hand on top of the Raeburn for support as she began to rise slowly with her shovelful of ashes. Then came the noise of doors being roughly thrust open and Fergus came bursting into the room. "Mum," he cried, "Jezebel's gone!"

Hannah wobbled unsteadily before getting to her feet, so dropping the full shovel, which landed on the floor with a loud clatter. Clouds of fine grey ash spiralled upwards before slowly drifting down to cover everybody and everything in the room.

"Who in all conscience is Jezebel?" exclaimed Carrie as she tried to spit the ash from her mouth.

"The cow! She's our cow!" wailed Hannah.

"But it's such a small island. She surely can't have strayed far."

"You're right there. She's not gone far. But that's not the problem," cried Hannah.

Carrie was quite mystified. "Then whatever *is* the problem?"

"The bull, of course," Fergus explained with a knowing wink at his aunt. "He was brought over two days ago to serve all the cows on the island."

"And everybody else's cow has to be dragged over to him; and now our Jezebel . . ." Hannah hesitated and wrung her hands, ". . . has actually gone seeking him! Oh, the shame of it! The absolute disgrace of it all!"

"Disgrace?" exclaimed Carrie. "How can a cow going looking for a bull bring disgrace on us?"

Hannah had no time to answer before a hen marched straight in and soon began cluck-clucking contently as it proceeded to lay an egg under the table.

By now the general hubbub had wakened the whole household and they had all assembled in the living room, just as the calf that Jezebel seemed to have abandoned poked its head around the door looking for its mother. To add to the general confusion, Sophie, who never could stand any offensive smell, became acutely aware that Angus, Hannah's youngest son, was urgently in need of his nappy being changed; and so, without a second thought, she diligently set about the task. The only difficulty was that she couldn't find any clean nappies and as soon as she set him down he began to run around the room, naked from the waist down.

Surveying the mayhem, Hannah clenched her fists, drummed them fiercely on her chin and without a word pushed past the calf and fled from the house.

"Where's she going?" Carrie asked.

"To the church, of course. To pray," said Morag. "That's what she always does when she doesn't know what on earth to do!"

Carrie gasped. *She* didn't know what to do either. Maybe she too should try asking God for some guidance. With an effort she managed to squeeze past the calf to follow her sister and was about to leap over her first boulder when she was halted in mid-jump by a most horrendous and bloodcurdling scream. Landing flat on her back, she realised from the piercing tones of the shriek that a child was in trouble.

Dashing back into the house she discovered that the agonised howling was coming from two-year-old Angus, who was now corralled in the far corner of the living room by the desperately hungry lamb who was prepared to feed off anything that resembled a teat – in this case poor Angus's little penis! Instinctively, Carrie swept Angus into her arms, stroked his back soothingly and kissed him passionately. Then, surveying the surrounding chaos, she realised that order simply had to be restored – and that she herself would have to take charge.

First, Morag and Sophie were ordered to wash and dress the younger children. Fergus was then instructed to get the calf out of the house and back into the byre before going in search of the calf's wanton mother. And once he'd found her, he was then to milk her, as the family seemed to be lacking in that essential. Katie was sent out, first to collect the eggs and next to feed the hens. She was then to help Morag and Sophie hang out the washing after their initial chores had been completed. Roddy found the naughty lamb being virtually kicked towards him by a now ruthless Carrie, who sternly commanded him to return it to the byre and make an absolutely secure home for it there. Carrie's final demand was that, when all her instructions had been properly carried out, they were to make a human chain and bring up as much water as the family would need for the day.

Once the lamb had been safely removed, Carrie put Angus down and set about washing all the dishes and mopping the floor before starting to bake soda bread, scones and pancakes. After that it would be time to fry up some breakfast. Three hours had passed, however, before the home was finally clean, tidy and bright. The whole brood of Hannah's children were happy once more – all, that is, except Angus, who had climbed up onto the window ledge where he could lovingly protect his precious manhood by fiercely clutching it!

The table was set and the smell of bread, bacon, black pudding, sausages and eggs had them all growing excited with anticipation. Carrie was flipping the last pancake when the door opened and there stood Hannah, pulling her headscarf from off her head.

The younger children at once hurled themselves towards her and made a tight circle around their mother's waist. Hannah patted each of their heads as she took stock of her home, the home that just a few hours ago had seemed so cold, miserable and impoverished, but was now as she used to have it – warm, bright and inviting: a place where children might know they were safe and loved. Hannah gazed at the scene before glancing out of the window where the dancing washing seemed to be waving merrily to her. As she turned her gaze back into the room, she was near to tears but sniffed vigorously before looking at her sister and triumphantly asking, "*Now*, my sister, do you doubt the power of prayer!"

Sam and his team had finally arrived on the island and were settling in. Fergus, who naturally assumed he'd form part of the construction team, had willingly directed the four tradesmen up to the Chapel House where they were to have their sleeping quarters. As Fergus introduced them to Father Donald, he emphasised, "Mummy says to thank you again, Father, for letting the men sleep here." Turning to the men he added, "But you are to have *all* your meals down with us."

Father Donald said nothing but bestowed a gracious smile on everyone. He knew just how much Fergus missed his father. Often, when Jamie was alive, Donald would look down from the Chapel House and see Jamie and Fergus getting the boat out to do a spot of line-fishing. Or sometimes Jamie would be teaching Fergus about crofting and how to be a good shepherd. Donald also knew that Fergus felt he should now shoulder as many of his father's responsibilities as possible – not only in tending the flock of sheep but in shepherding his mother and siblings too.

Fergus had just departed with the men when Carrie asked Sam, as she made a pot of tea, "How are things back at home?"

"Fine. Will and I had three good days out golfing together. But he's away back to work now," replied Sam, looking shrewdly about the room, "and talking of work – you've been here for a whole week now and what have *you* accomplished?"

Carrie felt she was a wee girl again and was being asked to justify her contribution to the household and its problems. "Well," she began hesitantly, "I bake and cook every day but there never seems to be enough."

"Huh!" said Sam dismissively.

"Look Sam, just you wait till you see what happens at mealtimes before you start finding fault with me. The NAAFI couldn't keep this lot going."

"Is this your way of telling me you haven't yet started on planting the potatoes?"

"That's right," was Carrie's curt reply, as she produced a scone she'd been saving for Sam. Deciding he didn't deserve it, she started eating it herself. "And since you're so ruddy smart you can join me tomorrow on doing the easy bit."

"And what was the difficult part?"

"Oh, would you believe it, just the gathering of the seaweed."

"And what was hard about that?"

"Well, first of all you wait till the tide goes out. Then you go down in the perishing cold with a creel strapped to your back and you gather the kelp up. Then, when the creel weighs about a hundredweight, you lift it on to your back and *then* do your best to climb back up to the potato patch, where you not only spread it out but nearly kill yourself an' all."

Sam felt chastened. "Look, I'm leaving the building work to the blokes who are experts, so tomorrow I'll be able to help you do the planting."

The household had breakfasted early and the men were already hard at work on the extension. Carrie and Hannah had cleared the breakfast dishes and were ready to join Sam out on the potato field. Hannah then explained how lazybed planting was done and it was evident from the start that there was nothing in the slightest "lazy" about it. First of all, she said, you had to dig a trench – but this simple task was impeded by the numerous gigantic boulders that couldn't be removed so had to be worked around. Then you spread some cow manure that had to be taken from the dung heap (which unfortunately was located at the far end of the croft) before you laid down an ample layer of kelp. And finally you laid in the potatoes before covering them with soil. Hannah assured them both that once ready for howking in the autumn, they would be so clean you scarcely needed to wash them.

Carrie's heart sank. It was going to be a long, laborious task and the wind shrieking about her was already chilling her to the marrow. Her spirits were further deflated when Hannah announced that now Carrie and Sam knew what needed doing, she would go up to the Chapel House to make the men's beds – and while she was up there and Easter being due shortly she would scrub the chapel floor as well!

"Right," said Sam as Hannah headed off, "you start digging, Carrie, and I'll do the hard bit and cart the dung over."

Two hours later Carrie's hands were caked with mud and stiff with cold. She did try to straighten her back but the effort resulted in a series of excruciating spasms that ran the full length of her spine, down her legs and into her very toes.

"Come on, old girl," Sam encouraged, while tipping yet another barrow-load of dung at his sister's feet. Carrie only groaned in reply as she tried desperately to straighten up. "You're not half out of condition, Carrie. I well remember . . ."

Carrie was at last upright and Sam's memories were triggered when he looked at her tear-smudged face. He recalled so clearly how, when no more than bairns, they both had to go to the potato-picking to raise money for the rent so that they wouldn't be evicted. He could vividly picture how her hands, as today, were caked with mud, her fingernails broken and edged in black dirt. The most poignant of those reminiscences was of dragging her from the sodden field and holding her close to him – just as he was instinctively doing now. That small act of brotherly kindness resulted of course in Carrie sobbing profusely upon his chest. "Oh, Sam," she cried, "if *I* can't cope with this life for a fortnight," and she gestured with a wave of her arm towards the croft and all its needs, "how is our Hannah ever going to survive? And the children . . . The last thing I want for them is to have a childhood like ours – a childhood where you were never able to be simply a child and play to your heart's content."

Sam let Carrie exhaust herself with sobbing before speaking. "Don't worry. Hannah will make it. She was brought up by Mam, and it will never dawn on her that the burden she's been left with is too heavy for her. Like Mam did, she'll just get on with it."

"Wish I was as confident as you, Sam," Carrie sobbed, wiping her tears away and smudging her face with mud. "Oh, I just wish there was some man who'd come along and marry her. Help her with it all. But who's going to take on nine bairns, bairns just like us with minds of their own – not to mention the thirty sheep, twenty hens, an insomniac cockerel, three ponies and a randy cow?"

Sam laughed softly while he rocked Carrie to and fro lovingly. "Carrie, she *has* remarried." Carrie looked up in shocked bewilderment. "She's now wedded to her church and no matter what happens she'll feel certain it will never let her down."

Before Carrie and Sam could say more, they became aware that an old man, carrying an even older spade, had arrived to assist them.

"That's good of you to give us a hand," Sam remarked.

"Och, what else could I do but help such a good-living woman," he said, making a little bow to Carrie before adding, "I'm Euan MacNeill who has spent all his days here on Herrig and never thought I would be fortunate enough to meet up with a true saint."

"You think my sister is saintly?" said Sam, quite mystified.

"Indeed, I do," Euan replied. "Because she is the *only* person, forbye the bishop when he was here last week, to be allowed to relieve herself on Father Donald's newly-installed con-ven-i-ence. So I said to myself that she could

184

only be honoured in such a way because she is a truly saintly and good-living woman."

Carrie let out a gale of laughter, grabbed Euan's wrinkled hand and kissed it. Sam too was chuckling but, looking at his sister, he said to himself: Carrie should always laugh because even though she doesn't have the good looks of Hannah and Alice there's something just so wonderfully engaging about her face whenever she laughs like that.

14

GOING FULL CIRCLE

"Headmaster," said Carrie for a second time, raising her voice slightly. Willie Hamilton reluctantly looked towards her. "It's just that you have two local residents still waiting to see you about the boys stealing from their fruit trees."

Willie sighed. "And how many boys are involved this time?"

"Just two . . . I mean three if we count the one that fell out of the tree and is now having his minor scratches treated by the janitor."

"And who is that boy?"

"Only one of the infants that Miss King enrolled this morning. Joe's his name – he's the younger brother of Wattie Scott."

"Are you saying we now have another of the Scott clan?"

Carrie gulped. "Y-yes. And Wattie did assure Miss King he had nothing to do with pinching the plums and said he had definitely told Joe *not* to follow him up the tree."

Willie turned away sadly and looked up at his beloved creation on the wall: the school's wooden shield, depicting children climbing trees, skipping with ropes and kicking balls; but most importantly, carrying the school motto *Omnia Neganda Sunt* inscribed in his own meticulous calligraphy. He had been headmaster of the school for less than a month when he decided that his own school, in keeping with nearby, up-market Leith Academy Primary, should have a shield and an appropriate motto. He had thought long and hard before he came up with *Omnia Neganda Sunt*. No one knew what the motto exactly meant, except for some of the teachers who had chuckled quietly when seeing it for the first time. On the day he had proudly hung it on the wall behind his desk, Carrie, who had no knowledge of Latin, asked him what it meant. Smilingly he'd replied, "Before I retire, in three years time, if you haven't worked it out for yourself I'll tell you."

Willie acknowledged to himself that his looming retirement was the reason he felt so down today. Yes, he thought: today, the very first day of the new school session, signalled his final year in the profession. He had come into teaching after being demobbed. Moray House Training College had a course specially created for returning servicemen and after witnessing the senseless carnage of war for five years he had felt the urge to see children being educated to think for themselves. Hence he decided to join the ranks of those people who might be able to do just that.

Now he had been a headmaster for ten years. At first it was so much easier for a man rather than a woman to be promoted to a headship; but things were changing and he knew that competent women like Miss King would soon see to it that merit – not gender – was the pathway to promotion. Being headmaster, he knew, had never given him the satisfaction that classroom teaching had. This was why he never asked for replacement teachers when a member of staff went off sick. He had always jumped at the opportunity of going back into the classroom; and until the teacher returned he would be in sheer heaven doing what he truly wanted to do – and what he was best at. That was also the reason he had persuaded Carrie to start studying and sit her O-grades. And she had passed all three, thanks to his tutoring her every afternoon when the school had settled down for the final period of the day.

Willie was still thinking about Carrie's continuing wish for more education when there came a knock at the door and Miss King entered. "Ah, headmaster," she began with a smile, "now that the janitor has tidied up Joe Scott, it would be of great assistance to me if you could see him first." Miss King hesitated before going on as she could see that Willie was distinctly reluctant to comply with her wishes. "As you know, the infants only attend in the morning for the first two weeks and he should be home by now." As there was still no reaction from Willie her voice adopted a more authoritarian tone. "*I* have calmed down the irate residents for you – so *you* only have the culprits to deal with, Mr Hamilton."

Willie sighed and nodded his assent. Miss King then opened the door and called Joe Scott into the room before departing, closing the door emphatically behind her.

Joe Scott was too small to be seen over the head's high-backed desk, so Willie indicated that Joe should come round to the side.

"Now, my lad," began Willie, "what have you to say for yourself?"

Without the least hesitation Joe piped up, "It wisnae me, sir. It wis some big boy who ran away!"

"And how was it then that you were caught with plums up your jumper?" Willie reminded him, pointing to the ample plum juice stains on Joe's pullover.

Joe didn't even hesitate before blurting out, "Yon big boy . . ."

Willie interrupted, "That would be the one who ran away?"

"Aye," replied Joe confidently, "but before he did a runner he pushed the plums he nicked up my jouk!"

Willie sighed and turned to look meaningfully at the shield behind him. Then, glancing sideways he noticed Carrie stifling a laugh. "You're amused, are you, Mrs Fraser?"

Still grinning, Carrie replied, "Yes, sir. You see, I won't need to wait now till you retire to know what the school motto means. I've worked it out for myself!"

Willie grinned. "Oh, you have, have you?"

"Yes. It's so simple! It's what every child who's done something naughty says when you ask if he was responsible for the misdeed."

"And that is?"

"It wisnae *me*!"

By the time the school had settled down after the short afternoon break, Willie was still feeling down-spirited. He knew he should have belted the two older boys who had been stealing the plums but he had an aversion to hitting children with such a cruel weapon – a weapon that hurt him more than the child he punished. Carrie's suggestion that he might like a cup of tea broke into his thoughts and had him thinking again about her educational future.

"Carrie," he said, looking across the room towards her, "now you have your O-grades, I was thinking that we should start on getting you a couple of Highers."

"But why would I want to do that?"

"Because all you need to get into Moray House are two Highers and an O-grade in Maths."

Carrie looked bewildered. "You really think I should go to teacher-training college?"

"Yes indeed," Willie emphasised. "Surely you don't want to be a school secretary all your life."

"But that's away above me. Besides, I'm very happy here at the school. Suits me just fine." Carrie could plainly see how disappointed Willie was by this, so quickly added, "But I will sit the Highers because I like English and Modern Studies."

Willie smiled. "Right, we'll start today and as we go along you may well change your mind." He was about to discuss what Carrie should be reading when there came an unexpected knock at the door. "Not another raid on the Victoria plums, I hope," he commented rising wearily to answer the summons. He didn't know who felt the more surprised – Carrie or himself – to discover that the visitor was none other than Sam.

"Very sorry to disturb you, sir," Sam began, removing his inspector's cap and tucking it under his arm. "I was wondering if I might have a quick word with Carrie."

"Something wrong with Mum?" Carrie cried in obvious alarm as she rose and joined her brother at the door.

"No, no," replied Sam. "But I must speak to you. Where can we have some privacy?"

"I'll take a walk for ten minutes," Willie suggested diplomatically and promptly left his office.

The moment the door closed, Carrie asked frantically, "What is it, Sam? Please don't tell me something's gone wrong for Mum or poor Hannah again."

Sam shook his head. "No. They're fine. But it's a problem that the two of us – or at least one of us – has to deal with."

Carrie slumped down on her chair. "Oh, Sam, you know I'm happy to do anything I can – but Will's buying himself a new car . . . so if it's money . . . well, as per usual I haven't got any. Or at least any to spare."

"Money? Oh, Carrie, when has money ever been an insurmountable problem to us?"

Carrie smiled. "I know that fine. D'you mind when we were just bits of bairns and needed to get the rent paid, or else be evicted?"

Sam grinned back at her. "Course we did! Some way or another, we always made it, didn't we?"

"Mark you, Sam, once or twice we even resorted to . . . How would a politician put it? 'Long-term borrowing' perhaps? Never *thieving*!" Carrie took Sam's hand as she remembered their daring youthful exploits.

Her impish smile disappeared sharply when Sam spoke. "It's Dad!"

"But what has our Dad got to do with us now?"

"Well, to tell the truth, absolutely nothing. But my friend, Father O'Malley, who's the only person in the Catholic church to know of our existence, told me confidentially that our Dad's in the City Hospital and that he's . . . dying. And not dying at peace, he tells me, because his conscience won't let him."

"So you're suggesting that you and me go and tell him just to forget it all and die with a clear conscience?"

Sam pulled himself up to his full height and he bent his head backwards so that he wouldn't see the deep distress on Carrie's face. Until now he'd been convinced that going and telling Johnny, their deserting father, that they bore no grudges and that he should go in peace had seemed the right thing to do. But witnessing Carrie's dilemma he became painfully aware that the plight Johnny had left his young children in was something he had no right to expect them to forgive. And if he was being truly honest . . . could he, Sam, forgive the cold, the hunger, the deprivation, the loss of his childhood and, most of all, the burden that had been placed on his mother who, despite her recurring depressions, was left to provide for the family even when the burden was too much for her? Sam inhaled as he acknowledged that his mother, though just in her late fifties, was already worn out, yet remained determined to carry on toiling for the sake of her family.

Carrie was whispering, "I suppose I *could* go with you to visit him because I don't want Mum burdened with it – but, be warned, I don't think I'll be able to say everything is hunky-dory."

Sam was relieved. "And what do you think we should do about Hannah, Paul and Alice? I mean – do you think they should have the chance to say goodbye too?"

A loud "Huh" came from Carrie. "Say goodbye to their father? Oh Sam, come off it – for Paul and Alice it would have to be a hello! And aren't you forgetting that Paul may be just round the corner but Alice is in Canada?"

"Yes, I know that, but Hannah was always closer to him than the rest of us."

Carrie shook her head. "No, she wasn't! It was just that she was older and so has more memories of him. Besides, she's done well these last twenty-one months since Jamie died but I can't see her leaving her children in Herrig just to come and hold Dad's hand. After all, he didn't find the time to hold hers."

Sam accepted the justifiable bitterness that was oozing from Carrie but hoped that she would mellow by the time they actually saw Johnny. "I'll pick you up then at half past eight tomorrow night."

"Half past eight tomorrow night?"

"Yeah. Father O'Malley thinks it would be better if we saw Dad after his visitors have left." Carrie looked puzzled so Sam explained. "Come on, Carrie, surely you understand. With him having passed himself off as a respectable bachelor, how d'you think he's going to explain about Mum and the five of us kids?"

"Oh, I've worked that bit out for myself. It's why tomorrow and not tonight that's got me baffled."

"Remember, Carrie. I told you last week that our police team is playing Hibs in a friendly tonight." Carrie gaped. "On Easter Road's hallowed ground, would you believe it, and I'm playing right-back!" Sam proudly announced.

"Right-back, Sam? You should try getting right back – right back to sanity!"

Carrie was almost finished washing up the tea dishes and Will was going over Sophie and Donald's homework when he had to stop to answer the phone. "It's Sam for you, Carrie," he yelled. Carrie came through into the living room still drying her hands and looked quizzically at Will who just shrugged. "What's up now, I wonder?" she asked, taking the handset from him.

"I've spoken to the Staff Nurse and told her you and I will call in tomorrow night to see Dad. The problem is she says he's pretty low. Doesn't think he'll last much longer."

"So we should go tonight?"

"Ideally, yes; but well, you see, I . . . I can't," stammered Sam. "But she says not to leave it any later than tomorrow."

Carrie was about to accuse Sam of putting his beloved football before Johnny when the line went dead. Then she thought: why shouldn't Sam go to his game? After all, he had always dreamt of playing on, rather than simply policing, one of Edinburgh's football grounds – didn't matter in the slightest whether it was Easter Road or Tynecastle – and if she was being truthful to herself, hadn't their Dad always put himself before Sam?

"What was all that about?" Will asked.

"Just that Sam's still going to play at Easter Road tonight even . . ."

"I know," butted in Will with a big grin. "Donald and I are going to the game."

"Though Daddy's not that well! Wonder if I could get Mum to look after Sophie while I go myself?" Carrie went on, fully aware of Will's enthusiasm for the game.

"Look," said Will, "why don't I drive you? I'll get Neil across the road to take Donald with him?"

"But you want to see the game. Couldn't I just take Sophie with me?"

"No. Like me, she doesn't even know him. So I'll just nip round right now and get your mother to sit with her till we come back."

"But I'd need to tell Mum why we're going out."

"So? It just means she'll find out tonight about your Dad instead of tomorrow!"

Will took Carrie's hand in his as they entered the ward. The night sister immediately came over and warned them that the visiting-hour was now past.

"Yes, we know," Will explained, "but we've come to see my wife's father – John Campbell."

The sister eyed Carrie up and down. "But his next of kin, his *only* next of kin, are his sister and brother."

Carrie was about to answer when Will coolly said, "My wife here and her four siblings are the legal children of Rachel and John Campbell, and I should be obliged if you will direct us to his bed."

Taken quite aback, the sister changed her tone. "But of course; and since he's terminally ill you have the right to visit at any time."

The guttural rasping of Johnny's laboured breathing sent a shiver down Carrie's spine. Looking at her father's emaciated body was causing her to question whether any desire for vengeance was worth having even though he had so cruelly deserted his family. There was no way that she could wish it on him, or on anyone else, that they should finish their life prematurely and in such agony. The handsome face that she recalled from her childhood was now so gaunt that the strings holding his oxygen mask in place had rubbed wounds into his cheeks – wounds that were now open and weeping.

Carrie had been sitting by his bedside watching her father uneasily sleeping for some ten minutes and all that time she could do nothing else but reminisce. Remember how difficult life had been for Sam, Hannah and herself. How there were those times, when Mum was hospitalised, that they were left without any assistance from him – the times when as raw youngsters they had to evade eviction by finding the payment for the rent, or scavenge for food, or stick cardboard inside their holey shoes, or rummage riskily on the train lines for coal. She looked at the man who was now sinking fast and wondered how, when he had deserted them, he had even gone into the bedroom where Alice and Paul, two defenceless toddlers, were cosily asleep under his Home Guard greatcoat and, without a second thought, had removed it.

A voice jolted her back into the present. "Penny for them?"

"Oh, Will," she glibly lied, "I was just remembering when we were wee and Dad was at home."

The voices roused Johnny and slowly his eyes opened. "Rachel," he gasped, trying to remove his oxygen mask.

"No Dad, it's only me."

Johnny squinted. "Carrie? Should have known . . . you see you're the one that takes after my mother." Carrie didn't speak until Johnny croaked, "Anybody else . . . with you?"

"No. Don't know if you know it but Alice is in Canada and Paul . . . well Sam and Paul are on duty at Easter Road tonight at some buckshee friendly game." Carrie felt it wasn't exactly a lie to say that Paul and Sam were on duty at Easter Road. Sam was there because he knew it was his duty not to let the team down and Paul would be in attendance because he never missed a chance to see Sam play – even Yvonne couldn't put a stop to that.

"And Hannah?"

"Hannah can't come. She just couldn't bring all the children nor can she leave them alone." Carrie paused before adding, "Like Mum, Hannah's children are her whole life and she'll spend that life devoted to them and their welfare."

Johnny sighed before lifting the mask to his face again and breathing in more oxygen.

"But she said she'd light a candle for you." Carrie went on quickly, thinking that perhaps she should offer her dying father at least a crumb of comfort.

A long silence followed. Then Johnny took a deep breath before removing the mask again to speak. "I'm so sorry for what I did. And I know you think you suffered the most," he hesitated before adding, "but you didn't – *I* did!"

"What?" exclaimed Carrie, unable to keep the incredulity from her voice.

"Aye, what a penance it was for me." He stopped to gather strength, then continued, "A real penance not seeing my ain bairns every day and having your Granny's condemnation. Could naebody see your mother was mad and I just couldn't cope?"

Carrie jumped to her feet. "Don't you, or anyone, *ever* say my Mother is mad. Okay, she has her bad times but she *never* deserted us and now, having slaved all her life for us, she's near done – done long before her time!"

Johnny struggled to speak. "All I want is for you to forgive me. Is that too much to ask?"

"Forgive you for leaving us to deal with what you couldn't? Sorry, Dad," she answered through clenched teeth, "I have the right to say that it's okay by me but I haven't the right to speak for my brothers and sisters – after all I just don't know how they feel about all that was done to them."

Johnny gasped again and the tears streamed down his cheeks as he weakly replaced the mask that was now his lifeline. But Carrie didn't see his anguish: she had turned swiftly on her heel and walked straight out of the ward. Will followed and when he caught up with her linked his arm through hers. "Could you not have let him go in peace?" he asked.

"Maybe tomorrow. But tonight it's just all too . . ." Emotion overtook her and all she could mumble through her sobs was, "What right has he to ask, tonight of all nights, that we forgive him?" Will knew better than to respond so she went on, "I mean, why did he have to get a conscience this late in the game?"

They were just about to leave the hospital when a nurse called out, "Carrie?"

Turning, Carrie found herself face to face with her childhood friend, Senga Glass. "Crystal!" exclaimed Carrie, hastily brushing her cheeks dry. "I didn't know you worked here."

"Auxiliary nurse, would you believe it?"

"Jolly good for you, Crystal."

"Well, I had to do something to keep my kids after my husband was killed."

Carrie squirmed. She should have remembered, since Sam had told her about the tragic accident that robbed Crystal of her husband. But here she was – a lassie who'd been so slow at school – now nursing, albeit as an auxiliary, yet sounding so confident and well-educated.

"And I did some O-grades last year. And this year I'm going to try for a couple of Highers at Telford College."

Carrie laughed and called, "Snap!" Automatically, both young women raised their arms and struck each other's palms triumphantly.

"I did three O-grades last year and I'm doing three Highers this year. The headmaster at Hermitage School thinks I should go on to be a teacher but I'm hoping to go up to the City Chambers to bag a promoted post there."

"Same here! A nice wee job with the Council and a decent pension at the end of it is all I need." Both young women smiled at each other before Crystal said, "But I'm so pleased you came to see your Dad. I recognised him right away – and with him being such a troubled soul I decided to tell the hospital priest the truth."

"What truth?" queried Carrie.

"Just that his distraught sister, your Aunty Ella, and her sons were not really his next of kin – that there was your Mammy and all of you."

The Edinburgh City police team that ran on to the football park for the friendly match against the mighty Hibernian team was the best that they had ever fielded. Even better, Sam reluctantly admitted, than the team he had played in when they won the British Cup way back in 1955! Their expertise was due to the young but very able forward line – five fit, energetic and gifted footballers.

From the start, all the fans knew that this match had been arranged primarily to give the Hibs side the experience of playing as a team before the real season began; but it was also an opportunity to allow the ground staff to check that all was well with the floodlighting – an innovation they were very proud of, being the first sporting venue in Edinburgh to have such a facility.

Very quickly the exuberant spectators realised that the young police team would be no walkover for the professional side. Five minutes before half time, a right-wing movement involving Sam at right-back resulted in a corner kick for the police team. Sam remained up field for the kick and connected with the ball to send it high into the net past the surprised Hibs goalkeeper. This unexpected setback left the Hibs manager reeling and he was thankful when the half-time whistle blew.

The second half saw some brilliant attacks by Hibs which were skilfully repelled by the buoyed-up police team. It was evident to all that the police side would probably be declared the winner and this recognition was so painful for some of the Hibs fans that they gradually began to leave the stadium. However, they were just spilling out into Albion Road when a roar went up – Hibs had eventually gained a corner kick and, greatly to the relief of their manager, the ball was headed straight into the net!

On hearing the loud cheer, the deserting fans dashed to be readmitted to the ground but were denied access by Leith Division's Sergeant Duff who announced, "You didn't want to stay when you were getting beat so you're no getting back in now they've half a chance of winning!"

Far from demoralising the police team, the equaliser only served to galvanise them to greater effort and they mounted repeated relentless challenges to the flagging Hibs defence. So great was their determination that the manager and remaining fans recognised it was just a matter of time before the police team would score again. A Hibs defeat at the hands of an amateur side was more than the manager could bear, so he promptly ordered the final whistle to be blown eight minutes early – due, he declared, to failing light!

It was nearly ten o'clock when Will's car pulled into Hermitage Park. They had made good time since leaving the hospital and their fears of being delayed by the match crowds had proved unfounded. Nevertheless, they were surprised to see Donald just entering the house as they pulled up.

"Donald, leave the door for us," Will shouted as he turned the engine off. Donald turned and grinned. "Good match?"

"Aye, Dad," replied Donald who, having been allowed to go to the match, was feeling quite grownup. "Uncle Sam scored first and it ended up a draw and Uncle Sam's team would have won easy but they were robbed because the final whistle was blown too soon."

The banter between Will and Donald roused Rachel who had fallen asleep. "Oh, you're back," she said rubbing her cheeks in the hope that this might waken her properly.

By now Will was ushering Donald upstairs to wash and then get ready for bed, while Carrie sank down on the chair opposite her mother. "How did it go?" asked Rachel, who had, herself, spent the evening in regretful reminiscing.

Carrie shrugged her shoulders.

"Nothing to say for himself?"

"Just wanted to be forgiven, Mum."

"So?"

"How do you forgive something that really doesn't matter any more?" Carrie lied. "Anyway you look all-in, Mum. I'll call Will and ask him to take you home."

"I'd rather walk. You wouldn't like to stroll with me?"

"Why not?" replied Carrie, rising and then calling to Will that she was going to walk Rachel home and there was no point in him trying to change their minds.

They had just made their way into Ryehill Avenue when Rachel simply had to speak: "Listen, Carrie. In addition to everything else that's been happening tonight, I'm in a real mess. At least, I'm going to be."

Carrie stopped abruptly. "What d'you mean?"

"Just that the blasted bakery is closing down."

"Scribban Kemp is closing down? But I thought it was doing well."

"No. Now that most folk, apart from me, have money to spend in the likes of Marks & Spencer and all the other posh shops on Princes Street, it puts the kibosh on wee second-rate businesses."

"So that's why you never bring any of the chuck-outs home?"

"What would you need with rubbish when Will brings you all the . . ." and here Rachel coughed ironically, "all the supposedly broken biscuits you'll ever need!"

Carrie ignored Rachel's reference to Will's new pal Fly Freddy, who was also the unofficial merchandise distributor when they were on night shift! "Forget all that," she urged. "There are plusses in everything. That job in the bakery where you have to heave all those great unwieldy trays in and out of scorching ovens is just too much for you."

It was now Rachel's time to stop. "You saying I'm past it?"

Carrie hesitated, wondering whether to tell her the truth or not. "You're not past it, Mum. But it's just not acceptable, now that we've all got on so well, that you're still having to do that kind of manual labour!"

"And that's the problem." By now they had reached the back door to the garages and Carrie assumed they would take the usual short cut when Rachel exclaimed, "You're surely not going to skip through that way at this time of night. We could end up murdered or worse."

By now Carrie had ducked through the small door and Rachel could do nothing else but follow her daughter. Not a further word was said until they were past all the garages and safely on to Restalrig Road. As they crossed over towards the Learig pub, Rachel raised her hand. "This is as far as you need to go with me."

Carrie didn't reply but sat down on the low wall outside the pub. "Now," she said, patting the wall beside her, "just you sit down here beside me and we'll talk about your problem."

Looking around in disgust Rachel snorted, "Talk about my problem while all the folk in that pub are half out of their minds with drink and thinking they're singing sensations? I think not."

"Okay, I'll just come round with you and we can do it at home."

Changing her mind, Rachel sat down on the wall and began, "It's just that at my age it's so hard to get a job. They're looking for young muscular folk." Carrie nodded. "And, as for washing stairs and doing other folk's ironing – well that was all right when I was bringing you up but now . . ."

"Forget it, Mum. It won't come to that. I'll speak to Paul and Sam and we'll come up with something."

"I don't want charity. I just want another nice wee job like the one I have at the hospital." Rachel sniffed. "Like dishing out the night drinks and blethering to all the patients. Especially helping the lassies that have just had bairns and don't know what to do with them."

It was after eleven before Carrie reached home but she was pleased that, even when on her own, she hadn't been murdered when taking the shortcut once more. Will was still up and more than a little surprised that, before speaking to him, Carrie went over, lifted the phone and dialled a number. Then she frowned when there was no one at the other end to answer. "Funny that," she said, more to herself than to Will. "Where might Sam be at this hour? It's not as if he would follow the boys for an all-night session."

Smiling, Will just shook his head. Carrie had never realised, or didn't wish to acknowledge, that Sam had become a different animal since Emma had ditched him. Certainly he wouldn't have an all-night drinking binge, but a couple of pints were the norm for him now.

Looking out of the window into her back garden, Carrie felt she had achieved so much that morning. As soon as the school had settled in for the morning, she had taken the opportunity to speak to Willie. "Mr Hamilton," she began, "I've been thinking about your proposal that I should study for some Highers this year . . ."

Willie swung round in his chair to face her, "And?"

"I think you're right. Quite right that I shouldn't be content to stay a school secretary. But I feel your suggestion that I go to Moray House and train to be a teacher is . . . well, honestly, that's a step too far for me because I really have no desire to do it." Carrie put up her hand as Willie made to interrupt her. "Hear me out, please. What I would like to do is to transfer to a promoted post in the City Chambers; and to give me the best chance of doing that two or three Highers under my belt would be an asset."

There was no response from Willie for a couple of minutes but eventually he said, "If that's really what you want, then I feel that's a pity since you'd have made an excellent teacher. But I suppose you'll do very well up in the High Street if you join the personnel department."

"Personnel?"

"Of course. After all, wasn't it yourself who argued the case so eloquently for part-time clerical staff to be granted the right to join the pension scheme?"

Carrie smiled. She had so thoroughly enjoyed contacting all her colleagues and persuading them to band together and demand the right to join the pension scheme – and also to have a retainer fee paid when they were off during the school holidays. Okay, they had only won a pittance, but she was certain that, as time went by, they would see an increase.

Having advised Willie of her ambitions, Carrie had then tried to ring Sam but yet again he appeared not to be at home. As it was his day off she found this strange – and she just *had* to have him go with her that night to see her Dad because . . . well . . . she realised that, maybe, she'd had something of a change of heart.

Carrie had just put the whistling kettle on the cooker and lit the grill when her front door opened and in strode Sam.

"I remembered," he explained, "that you usually came over at lunch time to redd up and snatch a bite to eat."

Carrie smiled. "Fancy a bit of toast and cheese?" Sam nodded and sat down at the small kitchen table. "About tonight . . ."

"Don't tell me you can't make the hospital tonight either?"

Sam shook his head. "I'm going this afternoon with Paul."

"With Paul?"

"Yeah. You see after the match last night I took myself out to the City Hospital."

"So that's where you were when I was trying to contact you."

"I'd thought I'd only stay a few minutes but Dad turned real bad so I stayed until . . ." Sam shrugged. "I know I should have called Aunt Ella to be with him at the end but somehow I just thought . . . was it so wrong for me to be with him?"

Carrie shook her head before saying, "Dad's dead?" Sam nodded. "Damn and blast! And here was I going to be so magnanimous and forgiving! And he's . . . Och well. Too late!"

"Anyway," said Sam. "Paul and I will get the death certificate and organise everything. We don't want Mum bothered with any of that."

"Don't suppose he's left anything?"

"He never earned much so I doubt it."

"Funny, isn't it, when there's a death in the family for any of my pals, they get left a wee something – but us, well, we always seem to need a whip-round to get our ain folk buried!" Carrie was silent for a time before saying, "You were all on your own at the hospital. Oh Sam, why didn't you ring and ask me to come and sit it out with you?"

Sam leaned back. "I wasn't alone. Remember Crystal?" Carrie nodded. "Well, she stayed with me till I got myself together and the Staff Nurse gave her time off to go home with me."

"But I phoned you again and again."

Sam's colour deepened. "Didn't go to my house – went to Crystal's. Nice wee flat she has, in Jamieson Place. And her two wee laddies are just great."

"And?"

"Oh, after the bairns went off to school – and they're both great wee footballers, believe me – I was all in, so Crystal made me turn in!"

Carries eyes widened. "You what?"

"Nice lassie she is. Come on a lot, she has. I'm going to take her out next week for a wee treat, so I am!"

"Good grief," Carrie exclaimed to herself as she walked up her garden path and saw that the storm door was lying wide open. "I must have been so upset about Dad that I didn't remember to shut it." On entering the house, however, she was confronted by Sam and Paul. "I see you've put that key I gave you to good use," she said, observing that both her brothers were drinking tea.

"We needed to have a family powwow," responded Sam.

"About what?"

"Dad's funeral, of course."

"Just arrange it all and remember to keep Auntie Ella informed . . ."

"That's the problem," butted in Paul. "When Sam and I went out to claim the body, Auntie Ella had already done that and insisted she was his next of kin."

"Here we go again," replied Carrie as she sat down on the settee next to Sam.

"And that's not the worst of it," Paul went on. "The hospital priest had a word with us and he's of the opinion that we should allow him to be buried as he's lived all these last twenty-five years. You know – as a bachelor and a pillar of the church!"

Sam took Carrie's hand in his, "His blooming church thinks we shouldn't even attend his funeral as we would be an embarrassment. Evidently the Abbot of Nunraw is sending a representative to honour our saintly and philanthropic Dad! And . . . och well!"

Carrie was bewildered. "You mean that we, his children, are to be denied the right to say goodbye?"

"Not exactly," Paul explained, with bitterness in his voice. "They say they'll keep a side door of the church open tomorrow night for us to sneak in to say our goodbyes after his remains are received into the chapel and everybody else has left."

"Say our farewells *then*," Sam stressed.

"But I'm for telling them to get stuffed and that we all turn up."

"No, Paul. Just let it be. We can do what we did when Granny died and go out to Mount Vernon when it's all over," continued Sam.

"He's being buried with Granny?"

Both Paul and Sam nodded.

15
AN ISLAND INTERLUDE

Carrie had jumped at the chance of a short visit to Hannah. Will and the children had gone north to visit his relatives in Smithton, near Culloden. Both Sophie and Donald were so excited. It didn't matter how often they visited Uncle Jack: they always wanted another trip to see the battlefield where, on the sixteenth of April in 1746, over the desolate moorland of Culloden, the last battle on British soil was fought out between the English and the faithful Jacobites. All too clearly, Carrie remembered the first time they had toured the site of the massacre and Donald being particularly anxious to know if one grave, marked "mixed clans" meant that was because they had all been cut up into pieces! By contrast, Sophie just relished the fact that her own ancestors – Frasers, Mackintoshes and Mackenzies – had been fighting on the Jacobite side. She was also pleased that Stewart Cottage, where they stayed and where Uncle Jack and her paternal grandmother had been born, was the first human habitation you came to when you left the battlefield.

Stewart Cottage, built just a few years after the battle, was full of relics from as far back as the 1700s and Uncle Jack had gifted some of them to Historic Scotland. To the children's delight, these were now lodged in Culloden Moor Croft House, which recently had been converted into a museum. Not only did the children have an in-depth knowledge of the relics there, but surprisingly they also knew more about the battle than any history book could have told them. That was because, when Uncle Jack had been a young lad, an ancient woman known as "Belle of the Battlefield" had occupied the house on the battlefield. So old was she that (so she told Uncle Jack) she alone knew the true story of the battle having had it from the lips of *her* grandfather who, as a raw youngster, had actually been present at the battle. Uncle Jack in turn had related all those fascinating battle legends to Sophie who thought it only right and proper that she should inform her teacher how wrong all the history books were!

Knowing that her children would be well received and entertained for a week, Carrie had thrown caution to the winds and bought herself a return ticket for the flight from Glasgow to Benbecula. She felt absolutely thrilled at the prospect of her first aeroplane flight – at least until she reached the airport and was faced with an aeroplane so small that it looked as though it certainly ought to be accompanied by its mother! Carrie's first thought was to turn back on the spot, but then she reasoned to herself: "Now, Carrie, my girl, you've paid two months' wages from your job at the school for this flight. That amount would have gone a long way to paying for a voyage all the way to America or Australia if you'd wanted to go there. No, my girl, you simply *can't* afford to waste all that money."

Having argued herself into accepting there was no alternative, Carrie boarded the plane and, as soon as the flight took off, began her personal relaxation routine in the hope of calming her nerves. Well before she had finished, the pilot announced they were about to land.

So desperately eager was Carrie to be safely back on terra firma that not only was she first off the plane, but had also gone straight through passenger control before the officers there had even taken up their posts!

As expected, Hannah was in the airport, eagerly awaiting her latest visitor. She always longed for folk from home to come and stay for a while with her. Every morsel of news they brought she would devour and savour as if she were at a feast. "What a surprise," she crooned to Carrie, throwing her arms tightly around her sister.

"Well, you know me well enough, don't you? I just had to come and sample those potatoes that Sam and I planted."

"Too late," said Hannah with a giggle. "We've eaten the lot. But don't worry. While we're here in Benbecula we'll do some shopping at their Co-op store. Much bigger than our one wee shop on Herrig." Carrie frowned, remembering that the Co-op here was really very small compared to what she was accustomed to in Leith. "Honestly," Hannah went on babbling, "we might even be able to get a wee bit of ham for boiling!"

On their arrival at Hannah's croft, Carrie was surprised to find a whole reception committee there, made up of Fergus, Katie and Myrtle. Before she could embrace any of the children, however, Fergus announced solemnly, "We are thinking you will be very eager to see the new facilities."

Carrie had to think fast. What kind of facilities were those? Then she realised she hadn't been to Herrig since the mains water was connected to the house and the bathroom installed. "Of course," she assured her nephew, "I won't even take my coat off until I've inspected them."

The bathroom was housed in the recently built extension, just on the left as one came in by the front door. Carrie was truly impressed when she stepped inside and was faced with a pristine bath, a gleaming wash-hand basin and – most important of all – a lavatory! "Well, well, well!" she exclaimed to all the assembled children who had naturally followed her in, "Is this not just too wonderful a sight for words?"

All of them grinned and wriggled with pride and pleasure before Katie announced – after looking to Fergus for reassurance – "Seeing you've not had the pleasure of flushing our toilet yet, you may do it now!"

Without further persuasion, Carrie firmly pressed the lever hard and, as the water gushed from the cistern and swirled into the bowl, everyone clapped and cried out, "Hurrah for our new facilities!"

Next morning, the two sisters had just finished washing the breakfast dishes when Hannah brightly suggested, "How about us doing a bit of shopping?"

Carrie was slow to make any answer. Having just arrived on the island the day before, the thought of dicing with death again by leaping from the pier on to the small ferry-boat that ploughed the angry seas between Herrig and Uist, and then clambering aboard the Benbecula bus where you had to do perpetual battle for a seat with hens, ducks, lambs and bucketfuls of lobster certainly didn't fill her with any great enthusiasm. She stalled. "But wouldn't we need to take *all* the children with us?"

Hannah laughed. "No, no! Not shopping on Uist. Here on Herrig is what I mean."

Carrie relaxed and ran her fingers through her hair. "Well, with your shop here the size of a wee classroom, the shopping should take us all of all of five minutes – and that's including the hike down the brae and back up."

On reaching the island shop, Hannah informed Katie-Anne, who had designated herself manager and was therefore in full control of everything, including the post office during its limited opening hours, that she'd bought a piece of ham when over in Benbecula the day before.

"Oh, then I'm thinking you'll be going to make the soup, Hannah."

"Yes. So I'll have a pound of lentils, a large leek and three carrots, please."

Katie-Anne pointed helpfully towards the vegetable tray, which held one very shrivelled leek and two gnarled carrots that were so old they'd started to grow beards. "I can give you the leek and two carrots all right . . . but as for your lentils . . . now, let me see . . ." and her eyes tracked methodically along the shelves ranged in front of her. "Well now, isn't that just too bad. I seem to have none of these lentils in stock today, I'm afraid to say. Alas, it looks like we're completely out of lentils today."

Giving a rudimentary sort of whistle to herself, Hannah stood there with a perplexed look. Since coming to live on Herrig she'd speedily discovered that, whenever cooking, it was vital to be expert at compromising and finding appropriate substitutes. She was just about to ask what she could have as an alternative to lentils when she was forestalled by Katie-Anne, who proudly announced, "But I did get some nice pasta shells in yesterday."

Hannah looked questioningly at Carrie for her opinion – and registered an almost imperceptible shake of the head. "Ah well," remarked Hannah, "pasta shells are all very fine in a cheese sauce but I don't somehow think they'd make an ideal substitute for lentils."

"Perhaps not," replied Katie-Anne, giving Carrie a distinctly hostile glare, having deduced that she was the reason for docile Hannah having grown so bold as to reject the pasta shells as a suitable replacement for lentils, "but yellow split peas are!"

"So they are, indeed," exclaimed Hannah with distinct relief. "So I'll have a pound of those, please."

"Well, you certainly could if we had any, but we're just waiting on them coming by the boat too!"

Fortunately, Hannah had no need to continue the debate. The shop door was roughly thrust open and Euan MacNeil strode in. "Peggy Mack said I would find you here."

Carrie, Hannah and Katie-Anne all looked from one to the other, wondering who he was addressing. "Now, don't you remember last week, Hannah, when the nurse went over to Fort William, you came and changed my laddie's bandages. And I was just hoping that you could come right now and change them again as I need him badly to be helping me with the sheep."

Hannah raised both hands in front of her. "No, no, Euan. I simply can't! Try and understand. It was all right for me to do some nursing duties when Nurse Flora was going away for a short visit to the mainland but she's back now on the island and it would look as if I was trying to steal her job."

"B-b-but," spluttered Euan, "she was the one who sent me to Peggy Mack's as she thought you would be there having your morning cup of tea and tittle-tattle."

Hannah had to admit it was quite true she had tea and a blether with Peggy Mack every morning but she persisted: "Why would Flora want you to have me dress your laddie's leg?"

"Because, when you're finished with my dog . . ."

"Dog!" cried out Carrie. "The nurse tends to your dog?"

Doffing his cap in reverence to Carrie, who he thought was a good-living woman, Euan patiently explained, "Of course she does. There's no vet here on Herrig. Besides, have you any idea what that robber of a vet on Uist charges?" Carrie shook her head. "Well, let me tell you that there's no way he would be satisfied with a fry of fish even if it was a fry of line-caught haddock!"

"You were saying, Euan, that once I have dressed your dog's cut paw I have to . . . ?"

"You've to go on to see the nurse as she needs your help too."

"Why ever is that, Euan?" quizzed Katie-Anne, who felt left out of the discussion and believed she had every right to know all that was going on in Herrig.

"Doubled up in pain she is. And she's too old to be having a bairn!"

Hannah looked imploringly at her sister, who knew without asking that Hannah was wondering if Carrie would look after the family while she went to the aid of the island's sick humans and animals.

"Of course you must go, Hannah. There's no one else who can help as well as you. Off you go with Euan."

As soon as the pair had left the shop, Katie-Anne came round and picked up the leek and two carrots. "I suppose then that *you'll* be wanting to do something with these."

Shaking her head in disgust, Carrie plucked up the courage to ask, "Would you have such a thing as . . . three family-sized tins of Heinz tomato soup in stock?"

On reaching Nurse Flora's house, Hannah was very concerned at discovering just how badly Flora was suffering. After a quick examination, she said, "Well I know you're fairly . . ." she wondered how she could say *obese* in an acceptable way, ". . . quite well-upholstered and nearing pension age but, looking at your symptoms, I'd say we've to get you into hospital as soon as possible. I think you have either got a gall-bladder problem or more likely kidney stones!"

Flora gasped and took several short breaths. "You're certainly good at this job, Hannah. Really good. You see, I do have a history of kidney stones but you didn't know that." Flora took a sheet of paper from the table and handed pointedly it to Hannah. "Now, see here. I've written down all you have to do today and who you have to see. And you won't need to escort me over to Daliburgh as Father Donald's going over."

Flora couldn't go on until a sudden spasm of pain had subsided. "And okay," she gasped, "the Father's not got much of a bedside manner but he's good at praying to sweet Jesus!"

It was well past lunchtime, and in fact nearly suppertime, before Hannah arrived back at the croft. "I'm so sorry, Carrie. Had to do all of Flora's duties. But poor soul, she's in a right bad way!"

"And what's up with her?"

"Kidney stones!" Hannah exclaimed. "Wish I could be wrong but I'm almost sure of it," she continued thoughtfully before adding, "but they'll know for sure once they've x-rayed her. Now, have you had your lunch?"

"Aye. Katie-Anne grudgingly parted with three cans of tomato soup and, along with toasted cheese sandwiches, all the bairns have been well-fed."

Hannah looked around her living room and glanced at the Aga stove. "And you don't have to worry about supper either," Carrie informed her. "I've got that all under control too. There's macaroni already in the oven – and chips just waiting to be fried."

"You're just a marvel, so you are, Carrie."

About to protest at this well-deserved compliment, Carrie was silenced by the arrival of Father Donald. "And how did you fare while doing Nurse Flora's rounds, Hannah?"

Hannah smiled. "Absolutely fine. And thank you for accompanying the patient to Uist. You know, Father, Flora is so efficient that despite all her pain she had my instructions all clearly written down – you know, who I was to see and what treatment I was to give them."

Pursing his lips in thought, Father Donald was silent for a few minutes before eventually saying, "You know, it's always been a great worry to me that we have no one available – no locum nurse – for when Flora's absent."

"So?"

"What I mean is, I think I should be proposing to the powers that be in Stornoway that, as we actually do have a fully-qualified staff nurse on the island who could stand in at a moment's notice, it would be wise to contract you to do just that!"

Hannah was dumbfounded. It was quite true that she was fully-trained and, having done her training much later than Flora, was probably more up-to-date in many respects than Flora. But, after all, she was a widow with nine dependent children, not to mention the croft and livestock that regularly needed her attention: so where on earth could she find the time to take on such a job, even if only on an occasional basis?

Sensing Hannah's reservations, Father Donald continued, "Mind you, there would have to be certain adjustments."

"Like getting rid of the cow? That cow needs more attention from me than all the children put together," Hannah complained loudly.

Father Donald gave a nod of understanding. Being rid of the cow was one of the things Hannah often dreamt about. There was all the feeding and housing of Jezebel, not to mention the hours spent tending to her every need – which included herding her up whenever she was chasing after the bull. That Jezebel had grown to be such a bind that life would be so much easier without her. And since almost all of the islanders now went to the shop for properly pasteurised milk, so also could she. Having a daily order for six pints of milk would moreover put her permanently in Katie-Anne's good books! "Well," she found herself saying, "I'd certainly enjoy putting my nurse training to such good use. But there's still so much I have to do here. And I'd have to be absolutely sure the children were well looked after."

"Oh, they would be that. I'll speak to the Headmaster about taking Angus and Ishbel into the nursery early," replied Father Donald enthusiastically, before rubbing his hands, slapping his thighs, chuckling and adding decisively, "Good! Then that's it all settled. I'll telephone Stornoway tomorrow and get their stamp of approval."

"But what about Jezebel?" asked Hannah quietly but firmly. She was determined to make sure that the problem of getting the cow out of her life was not forgotten.

"Oh, Gregor McGregor on Uist is always looking for productive cows that he can milk dry. I know he'll gladly take her."

"Aye, Father, that might suit you and Hannah," remarked Carrie, who felt the cow (of whom she'd grown particularly fond) was getting something of a raw deal, "but will Jezebel be happy with that arrangement?"

"No problem! She'll believe she's died and gone to heaven!"

Hannah smiled before agreeing, "Of course, you're absolutely right there, Father."

"He is?" questioned a bemused Carrie.

"He sure is that! Because hasn't Gregor got Jezebel's adored bull housed on his very own croft?"

By the time Carrie was due to leave for Edinburgh, Hannah was still having nagging doubts about standing in for the District Nurse. Training on the job had been suggested and she was keen about that. Yet she continued to be uncertain.

"Look, Hannah," Carrie grumbled when she saw her sister going into one of her dithery moods, "the children won't always be young and by the time they've all flown the nest and Flora has retired you could end up being the nurse here. And just think of the added bonus!"

"What added bonus is that?" asked Hannah incredulously.

"Mum being so cock-a-hoop when she realises that all the sacrifice she made to educate you and put you through your training is finally going to pay off!"

"You're right, Carrie." Hannah hesitated before adding, "But don't say a word to Mum – just in case."

"In case of what?"

Hannah shrugged. "In case Stornoway doesn't give its approval or, what's more likely, that I take cold feet!"

16
GRAND FINALE

Sam was giving a quick brush to his uniform jacket before hanging it in the cupboard when a sharp knock at his office door had him call out briskly, "Come in." The unexpected appearance of Pimpernel Pete, however, led to a groan of, "Oh no!"

Pete raised his hand. "I know, I know. With the disciplinary hearing tomorrow I shouldnae be talking to you but . . ."

"No, you certainly shouldn't!" Sam replied sharply, seating himself behind his desk with an official air that he thought would indicate to Pete that he was to be kept firmly in line.

"Look, Sam," began Pete. "We've been mates for years." Sam said nothing but bent his head, unwilling to let Pete see how upset he was at being selected to chair the panel at Pete's forthcoming disciplinary hearing. Pete coughed awkwardly before going on. "So I thought I would put you out of your agony and tell you there won't be any need for the hearing tomorrow."

Sam's head shot up. "What?"

"I've put my ticket in!"

"You've resigned?" Sam exclaimed incredulously. "But even if it *is* proved that you've been . . . er . . ."

"Fornicating with a married woman?"

"Whatever. You'll not be fired for that tomorrow – just fined – so why throw a full thirty-year pension away?"

"I've had enough. Besides, living in a broken down caravan . . ."

Sam shook his head wearily and continued for him, ". . . that has no sanitation and is illegally parked on waste ground in Salamander Street."

Pete scratched his head. "You knew about that?"

"Of course I did, but rather than have to pull you in myself, I decided on taking a blind eye approach."

Pete feigned a cough and chuckled. "Not much gets past you." Sam nodded in agreement. "Anyway, what I reckon is that I've now got twenty-five years in and that'll give me half-pension right away and, well, I've got quite a few irons in the fire where other jobs are concerned."

Sam smiled. When was it that Pete didn't have a few irons in the fire? In fact, he had so many that Sam was sure he should have been a part-time blacksmith. "And why this decision now?"

"Ken the pert wee blonde they all say I'm chasing? Well, I *do* see her every chance I have because . . . I can't . . ." Pete circled his head and rolled his eyes. "Would you believe it? The guy with a woman on every street corner just cannae live without this one!" He paused and looked down at his hands before adding, "And when I decided to stop lying to Sheila and told her I would be leaving next month, her answer was to pick up her gutting knife and –" Pete held out his right hand which showed a long angry wound.

"Must be real expert at filleting, your dear Sheila," said Sam with a sigh.

Pete continued, "I decided it wouldn't be in my best inter-ests to be castrated. Better to leave there and then."

"I accept that . . . but couldn't you have moved in with your Mum – on a temporary basis?"

Pete chuckled. "Move in with my Mammy? Nae chance! She's one of the old school. Can you no just hear her say,

'You made your ain bed so now lie on it.' No, Sam. The caravan was the only place I could find refuge."

"And your future plans?"

Pete's face turned red before blurting out the next words: "Jinty's leaving Alex and the two of us will . . . will really try and make a go of it." Sam sat dumbfounded as Pete remonstrated: "Try and understand. Jinty makes me feel just wonderful. She's all I ever wanted in a woman. Everything a woman should be – beautiful, brilliant company, energetic and – what's the word?"

"Charismatic?" suggested Sam.

"Aye, that's it – charismatic." A very long pause followed. "Of course you wouldn't understand, Sam. Women don't rule *your* head."

Sam shook his head at that. Since his father's death six weeks ago, he had somehow found himself becoming increasingly close to Crystal Glass and her two sons. Any day that he didn't see them, the sun didn't shine. And what was he going to do about it? Of course he knew perfectly well what he hoped to do – but he'd need to find out whether Crystal felt the same way. Biting his lip, he thought – what if she gives me a dizzy just like Emma had done? Dear Emma, who once had been *his* Jinty.

"Quite sure you're doing the right thing?" he reluctantly asked Pete. "If anyone should know about these things, it's me – that being head over heels for a girl isn't everything and that it doesn't always last."

Pete looked warily round the room, whose walls he was sure had ears, before saying in no more than a whisper, "I'm more than sure, pal. And I know passion cools, but with Jinty, if and when it wanes, we'll be lucky enough to be left with love!" Then, changing the subject abruptly, Pete suggested, "How about a pint? We can talk freer out o this place."

"Only wish I could," replied Sam, "but I'm already late for an important, *very* important family powwow."

When Sam arrived at Learig Close, all the family, with the exception of Alice, were already assembled. The happy sight made him beam with pleasure. There was something so heart-warming when they were all together in the house they'd been brought up in. Berating himself for being so sentimental, he focused his eyes on Hannah. "Great to see you, kid," he chuckled. "But you've only got two of your brood with you. Where's the rest?" he went on, unable to hide his disappointment.

"At school. But Father Donald arranged for them to be looked after while I took a wee break," replied Hannah, not admitting Carrie had told her that Rachel was completely exhausted and threatening to go out and scrub stairs now the bakery had closed. That was the true reason she had come – to reassure her mother that she was indeed going to take on the post of relief District Nurse on Herrig, which meant she wouldn't need to be helped out financially any longer. "Peggy Mack is looking after four of them," she went on quickly, lifting her youngest one, Ishbel, on to her knee, "and Katie-Mary was volunteered by Father Donald to take on the other two."

Sam laughed. "The good Father Donald is very persuasive!"

Rachel stood up. "I'll put the kettle on," she said. "You'll all be staying a while?"

"We have to," replied Paul, "Sam apparently has something urgent he needs to discuss with us."

"That's right," agreed Sam, walking across to take up his stance in front of the unlit fire. "Perhaps we should get that business out of the way first." Motioning to his mother to sit down again, he cleared his throat. "Ahem. As we all know, Dad died six weeks ago. Well, yesterday Father O'Malley came to see me because a problem has arisen that will need . . ." he hesitated and looked directly at his mother, ". . . a fair bit of tolerance and understanding."

"Tolerance and understanding? Is that your fancy way of saying there's going to be trouble ahead?" Carrie butted in.

"Yes, it is. You see, Father O'Malley said that Aunt Ella asked him to intercede with us because – well, because she can't pay the funeral expenses."

"Don't tell me she's got the nerve to expect *us* to pay?"

"Yes and no, Carrie. You see, Dad left more than enough to cover his funeral but it's sitting there in a bank book with his name on it – and, since he left no will, it needs the sheriff court to say who actually *is* his next of kin. And because a legal wife takes precedence over everybody else, it means that you, Mum, will inherit the proceeds of Dad's bank book. But you'll also be responsible for settling the funeral expenses and any other debts."

Rachel laughed as she stood up momentarily and then sat down again. "You're telling us Saint Ella even tried to have herself declared his legal heir?"

"Correct. But now she knows she can't beat the law," replied Sam. "So I'll do everything legally, Mum, and you'll be declared his next of kin. Once that's done, and you have the money, we'll be able to pay all the bills." Sam took a sheaf of papers from his inside pocket and handed them to his mother.

224

No one broke the silence while Rachel scanned the papers – not even when a frown crossed her face as she carefully scrutinised one hand-written bill. "The expenses of the undertaker, Sam," she said slowly, still carefully examining each document but gaining confidence as she realised the ball was in her court. "These are okay by me but . . . does she *really* expect me to pay for this insulting intimation in the *Evening News* that completely ignores the existence of all of you – his own children?"

"Mum," said Paul, who didn't want any adverse publicity to be washing over him. "Is there enough to pay it all?"

"More than enough," Sam replied. "In fact, there'll be a tidy wee sum left over when everything's been settled."

"Oh, just a minute, Sam," Rachel intervened. "This isn't about money. It's a matter of principle. And as she said . . ."

"No, Mum, we don't go down her road. Pay it."

"And will I also pay this, Paul?" exploded Rachel, tossing the hand-written account to him.

"So she wants the money for the boiled ham tea, the tombstone inscription, the . . ."

"That'll be the one that doesn't mention our existence!"

"Quite so, Carrie," Paul responded curtly. "And don't let's forget the wreath. Please, though, let *us* keep our dignity and pay it all!"

Hannah handed Ishbel to Sam before going over to sit on the arm of her mother's chair. "Mum," she said quietly. "Give her what she needs – but no more than that."

"You're right, Hannah," said Carrie. "Know something, Mum? A new teacher came into the school this week and we got blethering. When she came to asking me about my family, I was able to say in all honesty that you were alive but that my father was dead. I didn't have to feel embarrassed or humiliated any more. He's gone now – and so should all the hurt that his desertion caused us. What I'm saying is, let's close the book now."

Rachel gave a quiet sigh, realising she was beaten. All her children were decent human beings with not a trace of vindictiveness in them. Did she really want to have them get embroiled in a family feud? Of course she didn't.

Eight weeks later everything was settled and a balance of two thousand pounds had been given to Rachel. She'd proposed to the children that she should divide it between them as she was sure that was what Johnny would have wanted. She acknowledged he was no fool and would have known perfectly well that by not leaving a will she would inherit. Maybe he'd also been aware that it would also leave his sister believing it was an oversight! The only puzzle left to solve now was why Carrie wanted to have a copy of Johnny's death certificate. Rachel had asked her straight out but all she would say was, "Look, I may be wrong, so I don't want to say anything until I'm absolutely sure."

Meantime, Rachel and her psychic friend Bella were enjoying a cup of tea with a little dram in it – just to give it some flavour – when Bella asked what Rachel was going to do with all that money. Rachel lifted a teaspoon and began thoughtfully to stir her tea. "Going to get rid of it as fast as I can." She breathed deeply and then exhaled slowly before confiding to Bella, "D'you know something? When the bairns and me were struggling to survive, without having a shilling to spare for a pint of milk and a loaf of bread, Johnny was amassing his wee fortune by saving it up – two, three, or even five bob a week. Oh, aye. Must have taken him years to hoard three thousand quid." A satisfied cat-like smile spread over Rachel's face. "But know something you can do for me, Bella?" Her friend looked up in expectation. "When you next get in touch with Johnny, will you please tell him I mean to blow it all in just one week!"

"One week!" exclaimed Bella, thinking how Johnny would whirl in his grave at that news. She remembered well how panic-stricken he got whenever Rachel was on one of her compulsive buying sprees – so much so that after deserting the home he'd placed an advertisement in the local paper announcing that he would not be held responsible for any debts she incurred. However, not wishing to remind Rachel about Johnny's qualms, she simply asked, "But what on earth are you going to spend it all on?"

"For a start, I'll get one of those modern gas fires."

"But there's something awfy cosy about a real coal fire, don't you think?"

"Aye, but it's a real bind having to clean it out every day – not to mention having to go out in all weathers to get the coal out of the bunker."

Bella agreed, thinking perhaps Rachel was right enough about the fire. After all, she was quite worn out with all the toiling she'd done to bring up her bairns. So all Bella said was, "And what else is on your shopping list?"

"Well," Rachel continued, trying to smother her giggles as she pointed to the gas stove. "A new cooker, of course. I mean to say, that one has seen its day, hasn't it? Oh, and a fitted carpet for the living room. And for me, I'll have one of these beaver-lamb coats – all the rage they are nowadays."

By now Bella was so crestfallen that Rachel thought it was time to put her out of her agony. "But that'll only take care of a few hundred. Now what on earth am I going to squander the rest on?"

"How about another wee drappie whisky to brighten up our tea?" suggested Bella, stretching up to take the bottle of Glenfiddich from its shelf and then liberally topping up their tea.

"Och, I can buy that and some more of these half-coated digestives out of my petty cash," rejoined Rachel, opening a paper bag lying on the table and bringing out a fistful of biscuits, two of which she passed to Bella. "No, I was thinking more about what you were saying earlier . . ." Rachel stopped briefly, being aware that Bella seemed perplexed. "Remember you said that you had been speaking to my mother and she thought I should go out to Canada and visit our Alice."

Bella brightened up and sat bolt upright in her chair before adding another two spoonfuls of sugar to her fortified tea and licking the chocolate off a biscuit. "Aye, so she did. Your Mammy's met up with Johnny – and by the way, Rachel, he's feeling a lot better now and no gasping the way he did in the hospital – and he was telling her he's real glad about the ways things have worked out. And he's hoping that you'll put the money to good use and go to Canada to visit Alice." Bella stopped and looked about her warily. "And he says he doesn't want you to go all that way on your own."

"Wants me to take someone with me, does he?"

"Aye," nodded Bella vigorously. "Mind you, it would need to be someone older and very responsible."

"Wonder who that could be?" teased Rachel.

But just then Carrie flounced in at the front door. "Mum," she shouted, "I've got great news for you!"

Rachel smiled. "And what might that be?"

"Good to see you, Auntie Bella. How's things?" said Carrie before answering her Mum.

"Oh she's just tickety-boo," replied Rachel. "Going to chum me to Canada, she is."

"Oh, so you've had a windfall too?" queried Carrie, who knew Bella was always going to save up the money for her fare but somehow all she managed to do was barely scrape through the week.

"No, I'm paying for her to go."

"Naw, naw, Rachel. I just couldn't hae that . . . But here, wait a minute." And Bella looked over her shoulder, repeatedly nodding her head and interjecting, "Thank you. Oh, thank you again."

"That was your Mammy, Rachel, and she says it's okay for you to pay my fare but I've not to be a sponger so I've to find my ain spending money!"

Rachel agreed to that. She had always felt indebted to Bella's mother who had taken her in as an infant when her mother had died, thus saving her from having to go into the poorhouse orphanage. Aunt Anna and her own girls were living below the subsistence level but for all that she'd willingly shared what little they had with her. Now Rachel was in a position to pay something back by taking Bella with her to Canada – Bella who so longed to see her girls once again and never did she imagine she'd ever be able to do so.

"Mum," said Carrie, breaking abruptly into her mother's thoughts, "know what?"

"No, Carrie, I don't."

"Well, remember that lassie, Celia, I helped?"

"Was that the one whose was catapulted off her motor bike when it skidded in Leith Walk?" Carrie nodded and

Rachel continued to Bella, "Poor lassie, ended up face down in the gutter with her leg turned the wrong way round."

"That sounds like a real terrible accident," exclaimed Bella.

"Not really," replied Carrie. "You see, it was her artificial leg that had got out of control so once I got her sitting up she just birled it back round again. Anyway, all that is by the by. Hasn't it turned out Celia is a very clever lassie. Works in the Social Security down at Maritime House and she's a real expert on benefits!"

"Here, Carrie, I hope you've not been saying to the lassie that I need charity!"

"No Mum, not charity. But," and Carrie paused to savour the moment, "didn't Celia discover with you and Dad never divorcing, and Dad always paying his insurance stamps, that you're entitled to a widow's pension and a back-dated one at that!"

"No! Am I really?"

"Yes, and that means when you get back from Canada you won't need to find a job washing stairs or whatever it was you were threatening to do."

"My, my! A widow's pension?" Bella cooed. "I've always wanted one of them things. Gets paid out every week at the Post Office and goes up every year no matter what happens." Bella shrugged her shoulders in resignation. "But wi' my Rab being so damn cussed and refusing to stop breathing, I cannae get ain!"

Quite flummoxed, Carrie and Rachel looked at each other for a full minute before Carrie said, "So, Mum, Dad's finally done something in death that he never could do in the whole of his life!"

"What on earth are you talking about, Carrie?"

"Just that Dad's death has seen you provided for. And all you need to do now is to keep on your wee tea-trolley job that you enjoy so much; and with the wages from that and the widow's pension . . ."

"At long last, I'll be on Easy Street!"